Gathering Fireflies

Mai Chao

I dedicate this book to the courageous individuals who make this world a better place: the educators, students, parents, and community members who encourage and inspire us. We are successful because you believe in our aspirations and dreams and give us opportunities to succeed. This book is based on many true stories.

ACKNOWLEDGMENTS

I am most grateful to the following creative people for their assistance, guidance, and friendship: Stephanie (Ritter) Sullivan, Andi Vogler, Kathy Hoyos, Mary Beyer, Susan Beauchamp, Allen Harris, Jeanne Halderson, Amoreena Rathke, Rita Muphy, Linda Watson, Matt Gordy, Dr. Bee Lo, and Lynette Prieur Lo. I appreciate your time, insight, and love immensely. My gratitude goes out to these phenomenal readers: Joe Grosskreutz, Cassidy Zahn, Michelle Lydon and Sabrina Service for being the first students to read the manuscript. I am indebted to Kao Vue, Chia Vue, Shoua Lor and many Hmong people for their bravery and wisdom. Their hopes and dreams are alive within the hearts of their children. Lastly, I want to thank my husband, Reid, for his patience, encouragement, and love.

Glossary

Baht: "Baaht." Thai currency. During the early 1990s, the currency exchange rate was 35 baht to 1 US dollar.

Hmoob: "Mong or Hmong." A minority group of people from Southeast Asia.

Kajsiab: "Ka-shia." Hmong spelling of Kashia (carefree, light hearted, happily ever after).

Kuv niam: "Ku Nhia." My dear mother.

Me Ntxhais: "May Xai." An endearment name for a beloved daughter (darling daughter).

Mae Nam Khong: "May Na Kong." Longest river in Southeast Asia. Twelfth longest river in the world. Many Hmong families flee across this perilous river into Thailand.

Paj Ntaub: "Pa Dao." Hmong textile and embroidery using (not limited to) cross stitch, appliqué, reverse appliqué techniques.

Qub Neeg Qub Siab: "Ku Neng Ku Sia." Hmong expression for someone who does not change easily: same person, same liver.

Tasseng: "Ta Sing." A district administrator in charge of 10 to 20 villages in Laos.

Zij: "Zee." A Hmong woman physically taken or kidnapped to be a bride against her will.

Mai Chao

Chapter 1

Kashia: Son.

I am a new generation of Hmong,

a hybrid of Hmong and American,

made from love.

Mom says fate brought them together.

Defying traditions and building a life,

accepting, believing,

forming friendship into love.

I'm so not ready for this

love talk.

My light brown eyes are

almond-shaped like mom's.

I am almost 13 years old and

stand awkwardly at 6 feet tall.

My dad's European genes

run deep within me.

Only one head length to go

to surpass my old man.

Today,

something urgent demands my attention like

a mosquito buzzing near my ear.

Annoying.

All I want to do is play basketball.

I do not want to think about National History Day.

Basketball.

Focus.

What to do for National History Day?

I hear the echoes of Mrs. Vogler and Mrs. Sullivan's voices.

"Research a topic that is meaningful and worthwhile;

do something other than basketball, Kashia."

Ugh!

That something is lurking in my mind like those

deep sea fish,

strange, bizarre, bottom-dwelling creatures

who do not see the light of day.

My thoughts are hazy,

waiting to break from darkness to light.

"Conflict and Compromise"

What should I do with this theme?

Pa Ying: Mother.

Culture

shifts

like the direction of wind

that propels a ship forward

in a vast sea of life.

Our dreams,

hopes,

happiness,

perseverance

define who we are

as we search

for a place to belong.

My parents,

the two most significant adults in my life as a child,

made lasting impressions in my mind,

to be kind,

honest, thoughtful, loving.

Most importantly,

they want me to remember and know that

I am Hmong.

Somewhere between middle and high school,

my dreams begin to take shape,

grow wings,

I want to fly

and find my own way in this world.

Mai Chao

I remember the Hmong in me.

I tell mom and dad not to worry about me;

I am not crazy,

just a Hmong girl with big dreams.

I cannot bear to live a life without hopes and dreams.

My life cannot be dictated

by strict cultural rules and obligations.

In America,

we become

Hmong Americans.

I no longer dream in Hmong.

My native tongue has grown rigid,

rusty with disuse.

I cannot live the same life as my mother.

I am not ashamed, but afraid.

Fearful of losing

my identity.

I work hard to chase dreams,

dreams that flash before my eyes

like fireflies on a lovely evening.

Imagine.

Still,

I think of my people.

I remember

the past

told at times by

my mother and grandmother.

Sadly,

they do not speak

much anymore of the past.

Yet,

I know they dream about it.

Our history travels beyond China.

***

The Hmong were

forced

to move

in order to

protect

their way of life

from ruthless rulers.

Our true origin is difficult to trace.

Oral traditions

open doors to our past.

Scholars and folktales

speak of a cold place where the Hmong once lived.

Perhaps Siberia

or Mongolia.

Time after time

our people fought back when threatened.

When they could no longer

tolerate or stand

their ground,

they moved,

searching for a place to be

free

with their own kin.

Our ancestors migrated to Southeast Asia

in the early 1800s.

***

My heart is light in America.

My sky is clear,

open,

no shadows cast by a past I only hear about.

Unlike my parents,

and tens of thousands,

less fortunate Hmong

who saw things that

no living soul should ever witness.

I am thankful.

My son is curious,

smart,

free spirited.

That's why we call him Kashia,

our hope and happiness.

His National History Day project is

opening a door for us to reconnect with

our roots, our past,

where we come from,

how we got to America,

my peace offering to mend a broken relationship.

Conflict: Being caught in the hideous, violent

Vietnam War.

Compromise: The constant tug of war whether to stay or leave;

finding that delicate balance

without remorse or regret.

In the end,

heart-wrenching decisions made years before,

another lifetime ago.

Will Kashia understand?

"Call Grandma and ask to interview her."

"Alright Mom, but my Hmong is not very strong.

You come help translate," he says.

"Bring your Ipad."

He dials Grandma's phone number.

She reluctantly agrees.

Saturday morning, Kashia will hear her story.

Mai Lia: Grandma.

Fall in,

out love,

change,

be good wife and mother.

All life I struggle be free.

Heart happy in America for children,

but

I yearn home.

Laos.

Kingdom of million elephants.

I remember rugged mountain, steep terrain,

river valley each time I close

eye at night.

Beautiful village distant dream.

One day I return.

Someday.

I remember Plain of Jars,

thousand year old stone jars

scatter across flat plateau.

Big mountain make me feel

small,

safe.

In Xieng Khouang province,

north central Laos,

my home.

Here I think about past.

Talk to grandson *Kajsiab* make me cheerful.

Constant reminder of change.

Daughter, Pa Ying frustrate me.

I still angry at her

for marry

White man we not accept,

against wishes.

Ruin family reputation.

Unfixable like broken porcelain.

That another story to tell.

I think what need say to grandson.

Heart unsettle like churning water

in Mekong River.

Ginu: Grandpa.

Having absolute power,

being needed,

providing for everyone

no longer applies here.

Just an old man fading into the background.

I feel like a 50-year-old child.

Years of change and hard work gave me

a deep crease between my dark brows

like the distinct mountains and valleys

I remember.

My tongue stiff and unable to utter words that are

foreign to my ears.

I know four languages in Laos.

English is a

friend and an enemy.

I drift in America like a lost child

and I yearn to see home.

I long to hear the night

thrum with crickets and cicadas.

Leaves rustle in the wind,

the fragrance of fresh-cut rice stalks.

My heart cannot bear one more day on the assembly line,

sorting for undesirable, castaway, rejected pieces

like me,

like our people,

without a country.

Still, I do not complain.

I have a family to feed and am thankful for

a roof over our heads.

Unnatural to operate a headless machine

without a heart.

Craving fresh mountain air,

fog rising to the heavens,

feeling real earth on my hands.

The earth that fed my family year after year.

How I have missed you

my precious, lost treasure.

I cannot come back.

Not to live.

The war destroyed everything familiar.

Someday I vow to return.

Those tumultuous years of war,

1960s,

still haunt me

every night.

Chapter 2

Kashia: Son.

Balls of crumpled papers continue to fly into

my overflowing garbage can.

Nothing but plastic.

Swish!

Basketball vs. Hmong history.

Help me James Naismith,

Mr. Inventor of basketball.

You had 14 days to invent this game,

a soccer ball, and two peach baskets,

in a cold Massachusetts winter,

1891.

If the game "Duck-on-a-Rock" inspired Mr. Naismith,

something has to inspire me.

I grew up,

reminded that I have

Hmong blood.

Maybe it is time

I learn about my culture.

Mom and Dad would be proud of me.

Mrs. Vogler and Mrs. Sullivan

definitely would approve.

Is this a Compromise?

My brain feels like a sponge that keeps on

soaking, absorbing, searching.

My story begins long before my time.

Tomorrow I will discover more about

Grandma and Grandpa's lives.

I cannot even imagine leaving my home

with only a few things on my back.

My life would be sad and depressed if

I do not see my house and friends,

only to start from scratch in a foreign country.

Must be kind of like going to another planet.

Everything new, different, and surreal

like in dreams

where only bits and pieces from reality come together.

Yet,

they found a way to raise six children.

My mom,

the oldest, rebellious one, is most successful

by American standards.

She worked hard to get to where she is now,

an artist.

I was born with many

gifts from both Mom and Dad.

But then, I have a mind of my own

like the free throws I shoot.

Sometimes it's a little luck, but mostly practice and

hard work to make them drop through the net.

Dreams are like fireflies.

You have to gather them before they disappear.

Fireflies belong to the beetle family

and live only two months in the wild.

Two months does not seem long to us,

but it is a lifetime for a beetle.

Time is relative

like how "cold" is different in summer than it is in winter.

I hear many stories about the past;

yet, I only understand a little.

My instinct says I will learn much more if

I follow my heart,

learn about my roots,

while searching for a place to

gather my own fireflies.

Mai Lia: Grandma.

Saturday.

"America a beautiful country.

Generous, kind people

held our hands,

help get through baby step days of lives

when first arrived.

Kajsiab, let me tell you story..."

Grandson has handsome face,

flat Hmong nose,

light brown hair,

almond-shaped eyes like Pa Ying.

See his face,

like watch sunrise.

He take small computer out of bag.

I apprehensive and rigid like

animal in danger.

Not used to attention,

be in spotlight,

take serious,

give respect.

All life as Hmong woman,

I sit background like invisible spider,

listening,

arguing in head.

How I desperate

to give opinions,

thoughts,

ideas.

"It's alright, Mother;

don't be afraid.

He wants to record and to hear your story,"

Pa Ying reassure me.

Tap.

Shoulders relax,

loosen,

like maple leaf ride gentle on soft breeze,

to ground,

end of life.

America, final resting place.

Will I see home again?

Mind goes back in time.

Almost 40 years,

I stand on shore between past and present.

Travel back to old world,

watch childhood over like movie.

Some events more memorable,

but always

see village clear as daylight.

Rolling hills, lush green mountains, villages high

toward blue sky,

chirping bird, singing cricket

greet me.

I do not forget.

No streets, only dirt footpaths intertwine like veins

connecting,

linking,

weaving us

to heart of survival:

villages, family fields, friends, wild jungle.

I, only daughter among

five strong brothers,

valued like precious jewels,

heirlooms.

My mother,

envy of village women with household boys,

soon they become men.

They believe girls less valuable;

I only daughter,

one understanding Mother like

no one else.

We walk hand in hand to garden.

She teach me to sprinkle seeds,

bury corn kernels, pull weeds.

My heart joyful and bright with

Mother and family.

I walk with sunshine on shoulder,

happy and carefree

like bird fly in open.

If only had wings.

I go farther than eyes see.

Lantern bugs,

spontaneous lighting,

glow all year.

I think dreams,

but cannot recollect them

from mind.

Dreams given by Mother and Father,

be good housewife,

be caring mother,

not be disobedient daughter-in-law.

My own dreams muddy and vague.

Hope is lucid, distinct, and pure in heart.

"How old you Kajsiab?"

"Almost thirteen, Grandma."

"Imagine me your age,

think getting ready for marriage,

say good-bye to childhood friends,

not live with mom and dad again.

You ready for that?"

"No."

This happen to me.

Calm December morning,

first day New Year celebration,

I wake up heaviness in chest like

anchor hold me under water.

Beautiful, young, innocent.

Mother dress me beautiful clothes,

black velvet shirt with satin navy blue stripes on each arm,

loose black trousers,

elaborate aprons tie at slim waist,

colorful purses hang on each side,

purple turban wraps around head,

French silver coins

dangle and jingle from aprons and purses.

Shhhha...shhhha...shhhha...

coins hit one another I move gentle;

villagers turn heads to see who making noises.

I belong to Striped Hmong.

We know each group by clothes women wear.

I have black and navy stripes sewn around arms.

Together have

5 Hmong groups,

18 clans or last names.

White Hmong,

Green Hmong,

Flower Hmong,

Striped Hmong,

Black Hmong.

Years ago,

Hmong ancestors fought Chinese and lost.

Rulers divide Hmong people five groups,

anticipating

not reunite as Hmong,

divide and conquer.

Hmong smart and strong but outnumbered.

Many left China,

migrate south

toward Southeast Asia,

1800s.

Shhha...shhha...shhha...

Jiggling coins remind me

cicadas calling love songs in early summertime.

My friend and adopted sister, Kalia,

come over;

hand in hand,

we walk to festival ground,

Mother saunter in silence.

She afraid separate from me,

torn away by powerful people.

Old woman ask no question.

Hmong way.

Only matter time before I face

marriage.

Ball tossing game:

throw soft cloth ball back and forth,

while sing folksongs of love,

talk fondness to one another.

Courtship game.

Beloved Peng Su cannot protect me from

staring eyes of other men.

Ginu,

stranger to our village, wanders over.

Silent,

mission only himself know,

deep in love.

His catlike eyes say,

"Mai Lia, I want you for my wife."

I avoid gaze,

glance past him to crowd.

Sensing my unease,

Ginu back away into shadow.

I feel intense eyes

pierce through throngs people.

I seen his face before,

large square nose make me giggle, but I dare not.

Words unspoken,

only glance his eyes in brief moments passing.

Peng Su wear stern, unhappy mask.

Being maiden and not his property yet,

anyone can approach.

He not like competition.

Day disappear as sun set in distance.

Pink and red streaks splash across

evening sky,

promise another joyful day.

We walk back home,

Peng Su whisper sweet words inches from

face,

visit later,

speak through thin bamboo walls near bed

from outside,

be one and only love.

Face turn red like ripe chili pepper when mother

cough in disapproval our closeness.

Peng Su leave soon,

awaken from unfinished dream.

Uneasy feeling return.

Mother and I begin evening meal,

green mustard with boiled pork.

I walk down to creek for water,

cooking, washing, drinking.

House have no water, no electricity,

family happy live with nature.

When house no longer in sight,

heart leap with fear

at sight of Ginu,

wait with crowd of men.

Fear, terrible thoughts surface in mind's eye,

I doom.

They *zij* me,

kidnap,

force marriage against my will,

drag away

be Ginu property.

Like thieves steal precious stone keep.

I run,

run,

run,

until flip flops break.

Still,

I run.

Men close in; I fight from firm grasps

like fish struggle from line.

I scream,

scream,

but no one hear plea.

Power,

force,

fate,

I captured fish.

"I will love you, my beautiful Mai Lia," Ginu promise.

"Stop screaming or more people will come see our commotion."

Yet,

I scream until they take me relatives' home.

Before I enter,

elder take live chicken make

big circles in air in front Ginu and me.

This marriage welcome ritual let

spirit be peaceful with Ginu's family spirits,

accept me into new clan,

against

wish.

Fate,

written for every

Hmong person,

like a letter.

Maybe fate choose Ginu be with me

instead of Peng Su,

one I love.

I thirteen year old,

like you.

Start life with Grandpa.

Chapter 3

Pa Ying: Mother.

Choices,

decisions,

empowerment,

dreams

for Hmong girls.

They grow as fast as sequoia trees,

sustaining 3,000 years of life,

one of the oldest living things on earth.

Skin as thick as their bark,

three feet from the core.

Our period of dormancy and idleness is over,

like the cones of these giant trees,

needing a dry period of heat

to open and release their seeds

for rebirth of a new one.

Our time has come to be

reborn

in our new home,

America.

We can dream beyond our imagination,

from hard work,

sacrifice,

and

boundless amity

if we open our hearts and minds to learning,

growing, changing, gathering,

and keeping our

fireflies

alive.

We can make our dreams

a reality before our eyes.

Until then,

I see mother and my heart breaks into

a million pieces like broken mirrors.

She is unhappy,

a captured firefly,

hopeless,

alone,

desolate

inside a jar.

No education,

opportunity,

freedom of thought.

I tell her.

"What you mean?" Mother asks.

"I will show you someday, *kuv niam*," I reply.

She has not experienced what life is like

to do things for herself,

she cannot fathom the concept of individuality.

"We" comes before "me."

All her life,

everything she did was

for the good of the family.

Even when lost,

confused,

afraid,

lonely,

everyone came before her.

She is a strong woman

with years of perseverance,

tenacity,

a powerful will to live.

"What do you mean grandpa forced her to marry him?

Couldn't she just run away?" Kashia suggests.

"She would be a disgraceful daughter if

she ran away, Kashia.

Her reputation

in ruin,

loss of face,

no man to marry.

Her parents couldn't accept such

condemnation,

even when she needed their help,

even when it wasn't her fault.

Even when she was crying, pleading, begging,

they could

not take her back.

Voiceless,

Grandma sat in the background

while they discussed,

deliberated,

decided her future."

"What? That doesn't seem fair," Kashia says.

"Wait until you hear Grandpa's story," I respond.

Ginu: Grandpa.

"No need to record;

I am just an old man talking nonsense."

"You don't have to worry, Grandpa.

I want to record your stories so

I can hear them when I prepare my project."

Tap.

Memories

appear before my eyes.

Some things are too difficult to share with you,

innocent child,

but who else will

listen to the story of the Hmong people?

A long time ago…

The elders from my village deem

my father to be the strongest man,

make him our village chief,

where he oversees

25 families,

settles disputes,

makes tough decisions with the council of elders.

I am saddened he is not here to share

the fruits of our labor from the

Vietnam War

that stole his life.

I remember

foggy predawn mornings,

chilly fresh air against my face,

watching the sun do its

magical spell over the mountains-

warmth, life, contentment.

Mai Lia is a beautiful flower;

I know she will learn to love me.

Life is changing all the time,

Mother Nature moving our lives forward.

On special occasions,

we go down to the lowlands and

buy salt or trade with Laotians.

Most of our lives, we live in

isolation

with our own people.

Our homes are temporary shelters;

the fields

we use to cultivate rice, corn, and small vegetables.

Two or three years we seek a new plot

for more fertile earth.

Slash and burn, our way of life.

Before the new year celebration,

new fields are selected

to plant rice.

We find lands that have many

earthworm droppings.

Do you know what they look like?

"No."

They are little pellets of soil which tells us that the

land has rich fertilizers.

Together,

Mai Lia and I

build our lives around the farming cycle.

The sweetest months of the year are

November to January,

when the temperature is cooler,

giving relief from the relentless heat and

providing countless hours to hunt.

In the raining season,

I am so

miserable.

And yet,

a necessity to sustain life like the

very air

I breathe.

I feel healthiest in the higher elevations

where the atmosphere is cooler,

fresher, and invigorating to my

existence.

Home to the Hmong people are the

jagged limestone

mountain peaks,

jungles, fields, plants, animals,

family and friends,

together,

laughing, telling stories, eating

around a hearth

after a long day of back-breaking work

in the fields.

I will make Mai Lia find a way to love me.

Mai Lia: Grandma.

Boys,

men,

men's world,

pillar of society.

I want reborn into one,

so not feel hopeless

as Hmong woman.

Ginu's parents not love me.

I outsider.

I most sad when own mother and father

no longer call me

Mai Lia,

childhood name,

only name I know.

They call me "Mrs. Ginu" as if I stranger

to home,

like guest,

a visitor,

not part of real family.

I daughter and must leave parents,

unlike boys,

family,

no matter where go,

what become,

they forever sons.

Voice silence,

hands tied like prisoner,

I struggle move forward

and let memories go.

Invisible walls

separate true family from me,

unbearable.

Constant ache my heart,

like bleeding wound,

I weep,

thinking dear mother,

sunshine warming my soul.

I miss her.

Fury and bitterness

flow in body like poison.

I think how happy

before Ginu take away freedom.

Life stolen by man who play society rules.

To avenge hurt and pain,

Peng Su

marry best friend Kalia.

Nothing I do bring back happiness.

Never see or talk to him since,

like forgotten dream,

put away in depth of mind.

"Peng Su doesn't love you;

I am the one who will take care of you.

Don't worry,

I will love you as long as I live," Ginu promises.

I burst in pain tears and drown self in sorrow

bad luck as

woman.

Mother-in-law

not love me like own mother.

Sulky woman hate me

because I not belong same clan like her.

Son should have pick girl

she want daughter-in-law.

Women.

Think understand each other,

but no,

they put down, gossip, ruin one another.

Work.

Endless.

I start day at five each morning.

Sometime earlier before rooster crow.

I build fire in hearth,

fill pot water and set on tripod fixture

above hearth,

walk outside and de-husk rice.

Mother-in-law and daughters

wake to warm house.

What?

Say again, Kashia.

Sin-der-la-la?

Who?

I not know her.

Mother-in-law grunt, give evil glare.

I pretend not see and move about hearth.

Cook

bitter squash with sliver pork.

Fresh steamed rice melt in hungry mouths.

Eat breakfast silent.

I pack lunch:

rice, cucumbers with salt.

Sun peak horizon.

Work rice field today

then corn tomorrow,

follow men,

while they whistle cheerful into wind.

Chop, whack, pull, kick

tree, bush, boulder,

anything out field so we can plant.

All morning we drenched, sweat from hard work,

harsh sun beat down heavy.

Lunch.

Everyone gather in field house enjoy shade,

rest sore bodies.

"This rice is not tasty at all.

Whoever makes this does not know how to cook.

Rice is too hard to eat!" Mother-in-law spit vile words out.

Face turn hot as move behind Ginu,

try hide.

"Stop complaining, Mother.

Mai Lia gets up early to make us food.

The rice tastes fine to me,"

Ginu speak my defense.

"You constantly take her side.

Who gave birth to you?"

She storm out field house,

try make son feel guilty.

He grab hand and gesture to sit.

"She's just an old woman. Forgive her rudeness."

Heart skip beat,

feel trust roots grow deeper,

he protector,

someone who love when no one care.

Ginu and I become husband and wife,

help each other get chores done to

spend time

gaze at stars

and watch lantern bugs light up beyond front door.

Just when everything with Ginu go well,

I hear sad news from brothers

dear mother not well and must visit.

Ginu say go after planting season

when rains come.

This mean months wait.

Heart yearn home,

Mother.

I wait with anxious current run through body.

I not enjoy travel during rain season,

muddy footpaths line with leeches.

I work hard keep busy,

be first one rise,

last one lay down.

Dearest mother taught everything

about be good

daughter-in-law;

someday I teach own

daughter same way.

Culture and tradition very important

to Hmong way life.

Finally,

day to leave come.

Cold rain drizzle as depart,

a day walk away.

Birds and crickets chirp high-pitched sounds

as if happy see me

on path to childhood home.

Day drag as Ginu and I walk side by side

uneven dirt paths.

I see brothers stand by door,

nervous

waiting.

I run all might.

"What took you so long?

Mother is just hanging on to see you, dear sister."

I enter house and notice first her hair,

tangle messy threads.

Mother used let me comb beautiful river-black hair.

Two months since left beloved home,

precious mother,

no longer same,

wither away like dried vegetable,

without sunlight and water,

without love.

Face pale as evening moon,

sad eyes speak tiredness, fear,

no hope.

Her job raise me become

good daughter-in-law fulfilled,

except she not live see grandchildren.

I gasp and dash into arms.

"Mother!"

Tears sting, pain, sorrow,

her smile like fresh air

warming

world.

She look tired like 100-year-old woman.

Not say much,

but manage with pain in face to say,

"Take care of yourself,

love husband no matter what happens;

he is your home and life now.

Come visit father and brothers when

I am gone;

I love you forever my dear daughter,

remember me in your heart,

no one loves you as much as your mother,

think of me when you feel no one loves you..."

Her hands and feet cold like ice.

She look me like last wish come true,

hold me tight in arms one more time.

I see corner lips curl up to smile.

She happy.

I feel grip weaker and weaker,

then arms go limp,

eyes glassy like fish.

Take last breath,

and gone forever.

I feel vacant hole in center heart,

aching,

mourning,

more crying.

Tears cannot bring mother back.

Hmong people say she

died broken heart or loneliness.

I not believe them and know she sick,

hide from me so I not worry,

want me focus living,

protect even at cost of life.

Hospitals too far,

too few,

too expensive.

Many years later,

I know she die from anemia.

Only if she in America,

doctors give iron pills to help.

I have same illness,

but I survive.

Silence and emptiness in heart

grow each day.

Not hear sweet voice

burn

inside me,

soak soul with pain.

Soon after bury beloved mother,

whole country broke apart,

turn upside down,

like angry demons throw fire into world.

Short time before

death and destruction,

something magical happen between Ginu and me;

two stars become one,

shine brighter,

luminous,

memories.

His kindness,

stand up to mother-in-law,

help with chores,

make butterflies in stomach.

Sweet words melt heart.

I learn love him.

Maybe we meant be together after all;

written in fate letter.

One dark evening,

high in mountains,

closer to heavens,

stars scatter like beautiful jewels over heads.

Ginu rub aching feet with cold water,

massage callused feet with gentleness.

I close eyes and

cherish precious moments happen seldom.

I blush in darkness
while think of mother.
I
fall in love
with husband.

Chapter 4

Kashia: Son.

In my heart,

I have made the right decision to look into

my culture.

At first I'm frustrated;

it requires more time and thinking.

Now,

no problem!

I am fascinated by their stories,

in awe of their bravery,

totally clueless until now.

Every Hmong elder in America has a story to tell,

a fountain of knowledge,

filled with courage,

expectations,

hopes,

dreams,

just like everyone else.

Except they feel like children,

unable to speak for themselves.

It took some time for me to realize

they must feel hopeless in this country,

no education,

no English,

no turning back.

More on this topic later.

In my research, I find

the USA's involvement in the Vietnam conflict,

just before Grandma and Grandpa's lives changed.

1961:

To stop the spread of Communism,

President John F. Kennedy and his advisors

decide that Vietnamese coastlines provide

strategic advantages

through air and sea power,

so they go in to support

a weak South Vietnamese government.

Violent civil war breaks out between

communist North Vietnam

and U.S.-supported South Vietnam for

control of the country.

Laos lies on the western borders of

North and South Vietnam

and is supposed to be a

neutral country during the conflict.

Communism

threatens to spread all over Southeast Asia.

The Americans

fear that this spread may cause

a domino effect

and have huge economic consequences,

especially when China is already

a Communist country.

The Communist North Vietnamese army

builds a network of trails along the border,

transporting troops and funneling supplies

to fight the South.

War and violence

spread like wild fire into Laos.

The Plain of Jars in Xieng Khouang province,

Grandma and Grandpa's home,

becomes part of the network of trails.

Hmong villages

lie scattered across the undulating mountains

where the trail cuts through.

1962:

Geneva Accords of 1962.

As Laos remains a neutral country during the war,

North Vietnam is already violating the agreement

by entering, supporting, and collaborating

with Communists in Laos.

Something must be done

to cut off supplies

from North to South.

President JFK orders the Central Intelligence Agency (CIA)

to secretly recruit highland fighters

to help US forces,

violating the Geneva Accords.

An army is born,

the Hmong fighting force,

a secret ally.

A Hmong leader is risen-

General Vang Pao.

Ginu: Grandpa.

Mai Lia's

cold and bitterness is melting away

from the sunshine I bring to her icy heart.

As we go about our days in the mountains,

war creeps closer to our homes.

We do not know when the violence and chaos will

reach our villages.

I recall the distinct sound of gunshots,

people scrambling and running from the fields,

our peaceful village in chaos,

black smoke curling into the heavens,

death and destruction

knocking on our doors.

The first time I see General Vang Pao,

I know he is a good leader.

Entering our village from the sky in

a large metal bird,

he is like a king descending from heaven.

Intelligence shines in his black eyes,

full of charisma,

skillful in persuasion.

Not a very tall man,

but speaks as if he is one of those

giant White men.

He addresses the council of elders with urgency,

requesting our help,

pleading for us to join him,

urging us to fight Communism

or Communists will come take

our way of life

and impose their hideous ways on us.

He says the Americans agree to provide everything-

supplies, weapons, money.

"If we lose this war, what happens to our people?" asks my father.

Vang Pao says Americans can

find a place for us to live, if we lose.

If we win, they help rebuild our country so we can

live in peace and have our freedom once more.

The elders debate,

argue,

discuss,

knowing they have few choices,

knowing they have to send their strong men

and innocent young ones

to fight

a faceless enemy.

Vang Pao

soon leaves our village to move to the next one.

This is his way of recruiting and gaining

support from his people.

The Hmong people are split into three groups.

Let me tell you a little about our leaders:

Touby Lyfoung,

a Hmong leader during French colonial times,

a close associate of Vang Pao,

French-educated,

works hard

to integrate all ethnic groups into

the Laotian nation,

but his efforts do not sit well with some Hmong people.

As *Tasseng* or district administrator, in the Nong Het region,

he brings tremendous hardship for our people by

placing heavy opium tax on the Hmong farmers

to benefit the French.

1938:

Lo Faydang Bliayao's father,

Lo Blia Yao, is one of the first Hmong to take

a leadership position in the

Lao government.

Prior to Touby Lyfoung's position as Tasseng,

the job belongs to Faydang's eldest brother.

There are differences and mistrusts

between the clans,

Faydang's brother is demoted.

Touby's father becomes the new Tasseng.

After a year,

Touby's father dies and the post passes onto him.

Faydang wants to be Tasseng and

demands that the position transfer back to the Lo clan.

It does not.

He grows bitter and angry at the Ly clan.

To fight against

French colonial rule and Touby Lyfoung,

Faydang recruits farmers.

He later leads his forces to join

the Communist Pathet Lao.

Lyfoung and Vang Pao

support the United States of America.

The elders contemplate which side to join.

Some want nothing to do with the war and

prefer farming.

In the end,

we give our allegiance to the Americans,

separating ourselves from a family feud

that has little to do with us.

That first gunshot

ringing

in my ear still burns in my mind,

strange

like the surreal sight of

airplanes hovering over our heads.

By the time we reach our homes from the fields,

bombs already fall-

lethal, giant eggplants from above.

Boom! Boom! Boom!

We grab what we can and

scurry to the jungle for cover.

My ears zing with an unfamiliar pain

while my heart is consumed with

a new fear.

Our beautiful land,

littered with giant craters,

unreal.

Earth and substances scattered everywhere.

Smoke, confusion,

curling upward in a grayish black line.

Our leader will rescue us.

Vang Pao sets up his

headquarter in Padong,

south of the Plain of Jars.

We turn into soldiers overnight

to protect our land,

our families,

our freedom.

I am thankful

to have a strong leader who will

save his people.

When the violence first begins,

Vang Pao orders a mass evacuation of

200 Hmong villages.

Women and children

stay in specific mountain sites.

Men and capable boys join and train to fight.

I am one of the tens of thousands of

new recruits who leave my family for days.

Mai Lia weeps at the thought of me leaving,

tears symbolizing our love.

"We shall be together very soon,"

I assure her, while my heart has uncertainties.

I refuse to dwell on the unthinkable idea of me

not coming home.

Hastily, I join a group of men to go fight.

I oversee a company of 14 brave men,

trusted friends and reliable neighbors,

15-45 years of age.

American and Thai instructors train us

how to use field telephones,

shoot guns,

use RPG-2 rocket launchers and

AK-47 assault riffles,

weapons that turn a farmer into a soldier.

Factitious, unnatural.

I harden my heart into steel in order to kill Communists.

American soldiers,

a few heads taller than

the tallest Hmong man I know,

dress in camouflage,

vociferous,

out of shape.

They can hardly climb the rugged terrain and

mountains of Laos.

When we climb a mountain,

we go straight to the peak,

do not wind around and around

to reach the top like the soldiers we meet.

We do not travel in a line or make much noise either.

Many American casualties come from

carelessness.

For every 10 to 20 Communists,

there is only one Hmong soldier.

We travel in small units,

more efficient and quick;

everyone knows the landscape well.

We do not have much ammunition to waste.

Our strategy is to strike and withdraw from the scene.

Still,

we are vastly outnumbered by the enemy.

My men and I

monitor Communist troop movements along the

Ho Chi Minh trail.

We watch

how many vehicles go by,

what types of things they carry,

and how many soldiers accompany the vehicles.

In a blink of an eye we are under heavy attack.

Grenades explode

inches from

a large boulder that protects me;

chunks of earth fly in the open air.

Guns ring like fierce mechanical animals

screaming,

chaos everywhere,

confusion,

fear.

Oh, the noise.

I become deaf momentarily

as if my ears are

filled with liquid.

Bang!

Whoosh!

Ta-ta-ta-ta!

Boom!

Ta-ta-ta-ta!

Boom!

Ta-ta-ta-ta!

Images of my family flash in my mind's eye;

I am not going to die today.

Mai Chao

I look to the right,

I look to the left,

and see my brave men die before my eyes.

Their river of blood

seeps into the desiccate earth,

moans of agony,

pieces of flesh.

"Retreat!"

My throat is on fire,

dry,

hoarse

from screaming.

I do not even know that

I am screaming.

Crying,

praying,

wishing

to be anywhere but here,

away from this nightmare,

into the arms of my love.

Mai Lia:

safety,

comfort,

the way life used to be.

While combat continues on the ground,

U.S. bombers join the scene,

dropping cluster bombs everywhere,

not knowing

who is friend and who is enemy.

B-52 bombs fall like evil stars piercing the earth.

The ground shakes,

earth collapses into gigantic craters,

wind screams violent,

deafening sounds,

turning my core inside out with fright.

Ta-ta-ta-ta.

My hands:

damp, clammy, cold sweat running down

my back.

We scatter into the thick jungle,

massive trees with moss-covered trunks,

twisted vines and ferns,

jagged rocks that cut into our skin.

We run for our lives.

The noises begin to fade, then eerie silence.

When we regroup later,

only four of us come together;

we know the rest are lost.

My heart is hollow.

I cannot forget my men,

their bravery,

gut-wrenching moans before death takes over.

Late afternoon,

light diffuses and stills

like the surface of water with no wind.

Night is falling,

and we know the enemy

no longer pursues us.

What am I going to tell their widows?

I think of Mai Lia, and my heart swells with

hope,

love,

affection,

the simple gifts of life.

We men cry silently and

are gently comforted by

the whispering wind.

War turns even the toughest man into a child.

We cannot wait to see our families.

Mai Lia: Grandma.

Wait,

think,

picture worst stories in head.

What if Ginu no return?

I not like answer question.

Women stay

anxious for

husbands come back.

Several days pass and no news.

"You see Ginu?" I ask men return from fighting,

heads shaking,

marching on to find families.

I wait.

Constant

Boom! Boom!

Deep, hollow sound.

How I loathe noise of war.

After burial of mother,

I no contact with brothers.

"Where they now?" I wonder often.

Fighting.

Feel hopeless and restless,

I weep.

Thousands and thousands Hmong squeeze

into limestone caves.

Thousands Hmong die from

starvation, disease, despair.

Constant smell in air,

death cries from living

soar to ancestors.

Our family survive thus far;

mother-in-law nicer.

People hopeful Hmong king coming.

General Vang Pao take us to

Hmong kingdom.

I want old days peace return.

I think dead ones that

not receive burial ceremonies.

How can they reach ancestors' land,

be reborn

without proper rituals and guidance from the living?

We move constant;

no time farm,

raise animals,

make clothes.

Rice from sky save us starvation.

Some say American drop them because

Vang Pao tell them.

Others say Americans friends and

help Hmong long as

men fight.

I only farmer's wife,

not know about Americans.

I want husband come home safe

alive.

I hear commotion and

step outside cave

in moonlight observe.

Heart leap eyes seek darkness

for Ginu.

Toward end group

I see man

with head down,

unlike happy Ginu.

When he look me with eyes,

I see pale face like deceased mother,

almost ghost under moonlight.

Mouth

open say his name;

somehow sound choke throat.

I run toward arms with light steps,

heavy heart,

I see sadness in eyes.

"What has happen?"

Ginu stare blank and

cannot say things saw with brave men.

I hold rough hand tight,

not force him speak.

Stale smell, unwashed, and injured bodies reek.

As if to clean dirty bodies,

light rain begin drizzle,

softly wash away pain, misery,

remind men they alive.

Lucky women return cave with husbands.

Others wait, watch, then

sob heartbroken like

rain pour from above.

Days turn weeks,

weeks to months.

Somewhere inside cave

woman grieve for husband,

for father,

for son,

for country,

for home.

We drift one mountain to next and

not stay long grow food.

Hard rice, medicine, blankets, salt,

sometime meat

continue fall from sky.

Air America, our hope.

Mother-in-law

stop complain about real hard rice.

I miss sweet,

fragrant mountain rice

melt in mouth like rain drops.

Now peaceful mountains and hills

fill with angry smoke

curl up thick, black ribbons.

I not recognize village anymore.

Kashia: Son.

"Grandpa,

is it true that Hmong boys as young as ten were recruited to

fight once many older men were killed?"

"Kajsiab, just be patient.

I will answer your question soon.

I want to make sure you understand our story clearly."

Ever since my interviews started,

I have not been sleeping well.

My dreams are filled with stories,

fighting side by side with Grandpa,

holding guns that are taller than me,

running with fear in the night with Grandma.

The sights and sounds of

war.

Terrifying,

gruesome,

unforgettable,

an internal fear that refuses to go away.

Hmong people are

tough, brave, and courageous.

I look at them in our society,

working hard,

trying to make a life from scratch,

after losing everything familiar to them.

How many Americans stop to

think about what the Hmong have been through?

"Grandpa, maybe they don't even know that

you defended your people,

your country

fought bravely for America

to earn a place in this country."

Ginu: Grandpa.

In 1962,

General Vang Pao sets up an airbase

southwest of the Plain of Jars in

Long Cheng.

Thousands of Hmong follow.

We are refugees within our own country.

No place to call home,

no food to eat,

no decent water to drink.

Our people in the wilderness.

We are at the mercy of

the U.S. government.

Tens of thousands of Hmong soldiers are killed

rescuing downed American pilots

in enemy territories.

Sometimes

entire groups of Hmong soldiers lose their lives

just to save a pilot,

defending American makeshift air bases,

attacking and ambushing Communist convoys

to slow them down from reaching

South Vietnam.

Soldiers gone

as if they never existed.

Only their memories

burn deep within those

who know and love them.

American and Thai men,

desperate,

turn their recruitment to

young Hmong boys.

Little boys like you, Kajsiab,

to fight their father's war.

Boys are snatched from their mothers,

abducted from schools,

shipped to a few days of military training,

and thrown into chaos.

Many lose their innocent lives;

only bodies return home,

where families

wail and curse a faceless enemy.

Greatly outnumbered and poorly equipped,

we are no match to fight the Communist forces.

April 1975:

I panic and fear for our lives more than ever.

South Vietnam surrenders to

the Communist North.

Americans soon leave their operations behind.

Communist forces grow in strength and advance toward

American military bases

despite Washington, D.C.'s strong effort to stop them.

May 1975:

The Americans no longer

provide weapons and air power for

the secret army.

They stop dropping rice and supplies from the sky

and leave Laos as fast as they come.

Americans are gone,

taking General Vang Pao and

a handful of his top military officers to Thailand.

The rest of the Hmong people are left behind in

panic,

shock,

apprehension.

No one knows what will happen or

when it will happen.

The air buzzes like hornets.

C-130 cargo planes come

but not enough to take everyone.

Old people cry,

watching hopelessly as

massive crowds of

younger, stronger people

push their way into those planes.

Many elders commit suicide,

not wanting to leave their birthplace,

get left behind,

or wait for the unknown to happen to them.

The finality of American planes leaving,

desertion,

abandonment,

the death of an ally, a friend, gone.

If we cannot follow our leader in a plane,

we will follow him on foot.

Somehow following our leader establishes

Thailand as a refugee center.

Days after the fall of Long Cheng,

panic spreads everywhere.

Detailed military records

left behind in the military base

help Communist Pathet Lao

hunt down Hmong enemies.

December 1975:

Communist Pathet Lao

gains control of Laos and begins to replace

old political powers with its own.

Lo Fadang Bliayao accepts a vice president position

in the Supreme People's Assembly.

Touby Lyfoung is captured and thrown

into prison camp.

General Vang Pao cannot return to Laos and

decides to go to

the United States of America.

Russian Soviet (USSR) and the presence of thousands of

North Vietnamese troops occupy Laotian soil.

Violence in Vietnam, Laos, Cambodia continues.

Pathet Lao moves in to wipe out remnants of

Hmong CIA supporters.

In a hopeless attempt to live with the new

Communist regime,

we bury our guns,

hide our torn uniforms,

and burn proof of our involvement with Americans.

Tens of thousands of Hmong perish.

More bombing,

more massacres,

more bloodshed.

Communist propaganda

targets the Hmong people,

calling us mercenaries and

wanting to obliterate our race.

Persecution,

reeducation camps,

torture,

ethnic cleansing.

We no longer feel safe.

In 1978,

Phou Bia mountain,

the highest mountain in Laos,

rising nearly 10,000 feet,

becomes our new makeshift home.

Pathet Lao and Vietnamese forces

attack and assault us to no end.

We find no peace and

dig up our old, rusty arms.

The Communists' mission is

to kill any Hmong they see;

we are homeless

being chased away like animals.

While Communists pursue us to no end,

we also face a different enemy.

US planes release yellow droplets from the sky,

suffocating anyone who

breathes the vapor.

Yellow rain

makes people dizzy, nauseous, vomiting,

diarrhea until they die from dehydration.

Everything,

from soil to plants and streams,

is poisoned.

We barely survive 1978.

By 1979,

we can no longer live in Laos.

Thousands of families descend from Phou Bia,

flee deeper into the jungles.

Mai Chao

We begin our perilous journey,

following the direction of

the setting sun,

to Thailand,

across the Mekong River,

where we hope

to start our lives.

Chapter 5

Mai Lia: Grandma.

Last days blur,

change

like unpredictable sheets water

that fall quick once,

then die fast as rain come

in monsoon season.

Heart heavy.

I cannot stop think father and brothers.

Somehow

I know see them,

be with them,

and that hope comforting,

powerful like food make body strong.

Life in jungle depress and dangerous.

We on guard every second

day and night,

run any moment when

hear gunshots.

Americans long gone.

Three families grow bigger as meet

other Hmong running like us.

Slippery jungle ground,

cover with thorns,

branches scratch legs like twisted claws.

Feet aching,

body hungry,

unsatisfied and uncomfortable.

Children cry soft with

swollen bellies as mothers

try calm pain to keep moving.

Babies drink liquid opium

keep quiet, sleep,

not give away hiding place,

or many people die from Communists.

Some babies

not wake.

Small accidents, out of love and need.

Sorrowful mothers bury

precious babes

with love

in shallow graves,

sometime bury quick under

pile leaves as run for life.

No children should

see or hear

tragedy of war.

War selfish, greedy monster

poison innocent lives with despair, misery.

I no longer look at dirty faces;

remind how weak I feel as human being.

Think about precious children

bring hopelessness to soul

like I feel for Ginu when force

to marry him.

Then,

hope

shine bright above head like stars

guide and light unbeaten path.

Somehow

relationship grow roots and blossom.

I have reasons believe that horror pass.

Our journey

slow, tiresome, dangerous, will end.

We rest in day and travel under darkness.

We lucky Ginu have compass,

follow pointing arrow like guiding hand

inside circle toward Thailand.

Several men have flashlights,

use them guide at night.

When batteries not work,

we stumble by

faint moonlight.

Pitch black,

gray shadow appear before eyes.

I look light,

any brightness to see.

Sometime see lantern bugs

flashing bulb bright.

Only hope keep us go each day.

Thumping hearts pound louder,

dizziness,

frozen with dread.

Feeling way in black jungle,

long days, difficult nights

without home is

slow, painful

death.

No escape when rain come,

huddle in groups keep warm.

I hate sound of rain,

raindrops fall on body,

constant thumping

giving no relief,

soaking wet,

cold,

hungry,

uncomfortable

all night.

We move one area to next, search food.

We eat insides banana trees,

bamboo shoots,

leaves,

shrubs,

tree barks,

anything edible in jungle.

Pictures search food and shelter

stick in brain forever.

Then come orange rain from airplane smoke,

orange mist and liquid

cover everywhere,

make harder find food.

Fumes

make people sick;

all want is close eyes for eternity.

Senseless death.

Survivors move on,

only find more death to Thailand.

One night,

through thick treetops, I peek small crescent moon

radiate soft yellow black sky.

A gentle whistle like nightingale drift our way,

sound half human,

half animal.

Men use communication on battle ground,

recognize whistler is Hmong person.

Still,

careful they proceed.

Communist Red Hmong

also pursuing own people,

us,

to kill.

Gentle whistle come once more.

Ginu and elders look one another,

decide to answer back similar call.

Long silence before hear another sound.

Soft, urgent whistle make sense

for in peaceful time,

people press grass blades against lips and

blow songs.

Atmosphere quiet, tense, then something happen.

"Are you Hmong?" come whisper.

Faint moaning from children.

We breathe relief, knowing many Hmong people

are lost,

travel in groups, hide like us.

"Yes," Ginu answer.

"Are you heading to Thailand?" one man asks.

"Uncle Pa Chao, is that you?" Ginu's friend asks,

recognize stranger's voice.

"Yes, I am Pa Chao."

Group of 10 families slow join ours.

Together catch up news of war,

whereabouts of families.

I discover three brothers still alive,

one dead,

father wounded.

"They came at us from every direction;

screams of wounded women and children

still haunt me.

Enemies waited for us in a valley as

we entered a clearing.

Your brave father and brothers were leading-

the first ones to be shot.

Our group was separated two weeks ago.

If I am correct,

your three brothers are in Thailand;

your father and other brother is

no longer with us," Pa Chao says regretfully.

I cannot be sadder.

Mai Chao

Somewhere deep beneath heart

aches

day and night.

Ginu wrap arms around me while

mourn quiet in darkness.

Strange, peculiar sounds of jungle

surround sorrow as cry for

Hmong people too.

Dawn approach,

cool air,

dampness of trees, shrubs, rocks,

only add misery, pain to being.

I gather strength and courage move on.

Stomach growl pain and feel

tangled like roots I trip from.

Women, innocent children

whimper as new day begin.

Remembrance of hunger,

fatigue,

fear return.

Bodies ache weariness.

We continue trek on foot,

prayers answer,

in distance lies abandoned Laotian village.

Empty, ghost quiet, no soul in sight.

We grab rice grains, fruits, roots to fill hunger

for few days.

At last,

we hear roaring Mekong River before see it.

Deep, loud sound freeze insides with coldness.

How we cross river?

Gunshots ring nearer.

I pray silent protection from ancestors, parents.

We come too far.

We not give up.

I not want die without proper burial.

Kashia: Son.

Mekong River:

12th longest river in the world,

27,000 miles long.

Thais and Laotians gave

this majestic river a respected name,

"*Mae Nam Khong*," which means

"Mother of Water."

The Chinese call it

"Turbulent River" for its fast currents.

The basin is almost as big as both

France and Germany put together.

"Is crossing the Mekong River

the only way to get to Thailand?"

I ask Grandpa.

"No, some fortunate Hmong families

know trails that take them around the river.

Those who have money

secretly arrange for

Thai fishing boats to

get them across;

the majority of Hmong families

swim the river on their own.

We have nothing and

no money to hire anyone;

besides we do not trust them.

We have no choice, you see.

Either we jump in the river and fight for our lives,

or wait

for Communists to catch up and slaughter us."

"Do you know how many

Hmong people died during this conflict, Grandpa?"

"We do not keep birth or death certificates in Laos.

It is rural country where

people are spread out all over.

There are no institutions to gather or

report information because

many people are uneducated.

Scholars estimate the

Hmong population before the conflict to be

300,000-400,000.

All I know is thousands and thousands died in vain.

Do you know that even today, in 2014,

there are still thousands of Hmong people

unable to get out of the dense jungles of Laos?

The Communists continue to chase,

refusing to let them join society.

Old hatred,

revenge.

New generations of children are

born in the jungle,

who had nothing to do with the War.

Still,

they are being

persecuted and condemned to death

simply for being Hmong.

To really answer your question,

I have heard of at least one-third of our people,

soldiers and civilians included,

killed.

This conflict changed our people forever."

Ginu: Grandpa.

I remember the night my father was

killed by three Red Hmong.

He refused to join them so they silenced him.

We cannot even trust our own people.

I can still hear crickets and cicadas

crying their songs as

flames engulf our house.

We manage in time to

pull Father's lifeless body before the

house collapses.

Stars glitter like

diamonds under a blanket of darkness.

Everything burns to ashes in my memory.

I chant a prayer to my father's spirit,

asking for protection and safety to

get to the other side of the Mekong River.

In return,

I promise to sacrifice

a buffalo

for my father and our ancestors' spirits

to feast upon in the spirit world.

The Mekong is not only long, but

parts are as wide as

two Mississippi Rivers combined.

The roaring black water penetrates dark fear,

cold like ice,

deep inside every fiber of my being.

We do not have boats, life jackets, or inner tubes,

just ourselves against

a massive, slithering snake of water.

I have no time to let fear sink in;

I must take immediate action.

Life or death.

Adrenaline and desire to live is so great that

I am confident I can take my family

across this massive body of water with

my own hands.

Gunshots are getting louder by the second.

My head races to no end,

hand gripping firm on my large machete knife.

Within minutes,

we decide to go to the riverbank to cut

small trees and bamboo stalks,

fastening them into rafts for floating.

We return to our families.

Thankfully,

the women still have

their long sashes around their waists.

The sashes are untied,

used to secure each member to one another,

while fastening ourselves to the makeshift rafts.

I silently make promises.

Heaven and Earth,

father and beloved ancestors,

please protect my family,

do not let any harm befall us.

I promise to sacrifice

a buffalo for your spirits

to feast on when we are no longer in harm's way.

I repeat these words over and over in my head.

Our group of nearly 50 people advance toward

the thrashing river.

Some families are swept away immediately

and disappear

into the violent, turbulent black liquid.

We gingerly enter the gloomy pool.

Fast, furious, and instantaneous,

we are thrown into

obscure,

churning,

swirling water.

Black as coal,

gunshots light up the night behind us.

Ra-ta-ta-ta.

Shouts from Communist soldiers,

terrifying screams,

more gunshots,

smoke.

I crane my neck to look and am taken aback

by the hundreds of moving heads in the water.

The shore is getting smaller,

as I notice fire light up the dark jungle.

Ta-ta-ta-ta.

Gradually, gunshots grow fainter.

Another dangerous threat

commands our attention.

The current pushes and pulls us in every direction,

like getting swirled around in

a massive toilet bowl.

I have two brothers

who lighten my load with their strong bodies.

Harsh breathing,

children sniveling in fright;

the only thought on my mind is safety for my family.

Everywhere I look, I see gloom,

little specks of heads bobbing up and down with

the fast current.

Pools of darkness surround us,

deep, unknown,

frightful and bleak

like our future.

Only the fear in my heart reminds me

I am still alive.

All at once,

we cannot see, but we can clearly hear

Thai fishing boats

zipping up and down,

asking if people have money to pay

for a ride to the other side.

From a short distance,

I can hear the Thai fishermen asking two families

for Hmong silver bars.

Valuable silver bars that took a lifetime to acquire are

handed to them in an instant.

One fishermen

says it is fine to climb onboard while the

other shakes his head and

demands more money.

I can see that greedy one gesturing

his dirty hands to the

silver necklaces tied around the women's waists.

The women shake their heads in protest;

both Thais begin shouting at the Hmong.

The women look at each other,

start to take off their treasured jewelry.

They hand their beautiful, heavy, silver necklaces to

the Thai men.

The men's rapacious smiles

resemble alligators grinning

at cornered prey.

Both men help the Hmong families climb aboard.

We watch in alarm as the boat zooms past us.

Splash! Splash! Splash!

Screams

fill the air as

human bodies fall into

the murky water,

and the river

swallows them into nothingness.

Everyone frantically try

to stay afloat and cannot help these desperate people.

Soon the Hmong families disappear altogether.

The two fishermen,

shameless,

put their treasures into bags

and toss a cooking pot after

their victims.

We simply watch in horror.

I taste salt running down my cheeks.

The now-vacant boat circles around and then

stops near our float.

"We can help you. Just give us all of your money," he says in Thai.

"Get away from my family, or I blow your head off,"

I reply through gritted teeth while pointing my

useless,

wet gun at them.

The sight of a gun is enough to

scare these cowards, so they back away,

move on to rob

another innocent group.

I continue to kick and paddle,

as a flickering flame inside my body burns with

boundless energy.

In reality,

I am exhausted,

operating on adrenaline and high alert.

All I want to do is stop all the aching pain,

the agonizing discomfort,

my body on fire.

I want to close my tired eyes and

fall asleep

in this crude, unpredictable

river.

After almost three hours of struggling and

resisting water currents,

I begin to feel a change under my feet.

Water feels shallower and

almost warmer.

My mind and body shatters like broken glass;

still,

I fight until I know we are safe on the other side.

Mai Chao

I kick,

paddle,

breathe

until at last

I feel slippery rocks below my feet,

then soft sand,

and realize we have made it across.

I thought I would not feel solid earth beneath me again.

The emptiness and pain at

the bottom of my stomach,

a constant reminder that

I am alive.

The moon is crystal clear above our heads.

I am shivering with coldness and

overcome by exhaustion.

It must be well past midnight when

we hit shore on the Thai side.

Men untie family members;

we sprawl out on the beach like fish flopping on land.

Gasping for air,

desperately in need of shelter,

barely alive,

we force ourselves to keep moving.

Hundreds of us gather around, but we do not feel safe.

After huddling over jagged rocks by the shore,

we manage to find tall, long grasses nearby,

drag our families to hide behind it,

and wait for morning.

Thai robbers,

Thai patrolmen,

covetous beings are all around.

We fall in and out of consciousness,

waiting,

waiting,

waiting

for daylight to come.

Moonlight is fading as

sky begins to turn pale gray,

then shades of light blues.

Birds chirp;

we are enveloped by fog and drowned by tiredness.

The air is damp,

silent like a deserted cemetery,

except for the beating in our hearts

that forces us to keep breathing.

When morning light breaks,

streaks of blue and yellow line the horizon.

People from Laos continue to cross

the Mekong

to join our growing group in Thailand.

When we see morning light,

almost 500 people gather by the sand.

Mai Chao

Men,

women,

and children

shiver in tattered clothing,

fearful, defeated creatures in a strange land.

Thai villagers living near the river see us

stumble into their villages in rags.

They heard gunshots

throughout the night and

have come to investigate.

The villagers give us broth and

build a high fire in the center of their village,

warming our shivering bodies,

waiting for Thai authorities to come.

The village chief says the authorities are taking us to a

refugee camp

in Nong Kai.

We live in many miserable refugee camps

three years before officially

settling down

in Ban Vinai

where your mother

was born.

Chapter 6

Pa Ying: Mother.

1982:

Ban Vinai refugee camp,

Thailand,

my happiest childhood memories,

the first 10 years of my life.

Ban Vinai,

my first home.

Four hundred acres of land,

built for 12,000 refugees,

becomes home to nearly 42,000 residents at one point.

Every inch is occupied by human activity.

The camp is divided into nine centers;

we make our home in Center 7,

overcrowded, dirty, filthy like the rest of the centers.

The community bathroom pits exude an unbearable stench

that spreads across the centers like

black clouds of filth.

The camp has

one small hospital and a school for children,

set up by Hmong leaders and Thai officials,

resembling a very crowded Hmong village.

Each center

has its own leader reporting to

a camp commander.

Several times a week,

large United Nations trucks

come from the outside world

to deliver meat,

vegetables,

rice,

coal,

milk for children.

Each family needs to have a

Ban Vinai number in order to

receive aide and food.

Our family number is BV00747.

BV numbers are like social security numbers;

those with a number are considered

"official refugees,"

those without are

"illegals"

who get sent back to Laos.

Every adult in the camp knows his or her

seven-digit number

as if it has been

invisibly

tattooed on his heart.

I still use those numbers as

passwords

for school or bank accounts.

Oh, Kajsiab,

let me tell you

the one thing that I dislike the most in Ban Vinai.

Noise.

There is a child crying next door,

a stray dog barking,

someone wailing for a deceased loved one,

a mournful death drum thumping,

couples arguing,

banging of pots and pans,

children laughing,

grandparents telling stories.

Constant noise like a spinning wheel,

up, down, here, there

noises everywhere.

Thick red dust swirls like

little tornadoes from a

strong gust of wind.

I cover my mouth with my shirt, but the dust

dances around

until the insides of my nose turn black.

Children walk around camp with

dry coughs and

scratchy throats,

choking in dust,

trying to breathe.

Hot,

merciless heat,

as if we are in an oven with a fan

blowing tiny particles everywhere.

The sun is not high yet;

my thin clothes soaked in

sweat from humidity and dry heat.

Rain.

The simple pleasure of life for children,

dancing under sheets of rain as

it cools our small bodies,

relieving us from the heat and humidity.

When the rain

slows down to a fine drizzle,

I stick my tongue out to taste the lovely droplets,

mother nature's gift to the world,

fruit from the sky.

Life in the camp is

homey and jaunty for children.

We rely solely on our parents

for everything-

the eyes, ears, and mouths

that protect us.

I have not seen the beautiful mountains of Laos,

nor inhaled the fresh morning air.

Mother talks about

the old country often, but

I can only imagine the green,

undulating mountains.

In the camp,

I love watching thick fog cover everything

in a cool, gray blanket.

Each morning,

mom and I wait in line at

the water station for our rations of water.

Metal and tin pails,

along with their owners,

stand in long lines,

waiting to bring water home to be boiled.

Water must be boiled,

or our bellies ache, or worse, have worms.

Grandmother and her young adult children are

Mai Chao

still in bed

when we leave our compound.

As long as I can remember,

I see my mom do every chore

for our family,

and I wish to be older so

I can help her.

She does not complain,

dutifully taking care of chores and children

while dad works on his jewelry.

She touches my head with love and

holds my hand tenderly

as we go about our

daily business around camp.

After the water station,

mom and I go to the Thai market to buy

chicken carcasses,

kale, bitter melons, and eggplants

for breakfast.

I am nervous going to the market.

I see Thai guards with their guns,

watching the people or mingling

amongst us,

cradling their M-16s like babies.

The camp is surrounded with barbed wire;

no one can get in or get out

without legal documents,

which are hard to come by.

We are trapped inside this place like prisoners.

By squeezing my mom's hand tighter and walking

closer to her,

I feel safer.

I want to believe that the sun-burnt

Thai guards can no longer see me.

Before I was born,

Mom and Dad

had nothing

in Ban Vinai but

themselves.

They move from one filthy camp to the next until

Ban Vinai is built to accommodate

large numbers of "displaced" people

entering Thailand from

Laos and Cambodia.

Her three brothers survive the jungles,

stay in the camp for a short time,

and leave at first chance for the United States.

They see this place as a dead end to their futures,

deserting it without a second thought,

seeking a brighter future

for themselves and their children.

America.

Mysterious,

contradictory,

land of the giants.

Constant fights between Mom and Dad;

Mom wants to follow her brothers, but

Dad wants nothing to do with leaving.

"Can we go to America, husband?"

"No. We stay here and wait.

One day we go back to our homes and start over."

Screaming, tears,

mostly tears seeping from her weary,

subdued eyes.

We run to comfort

our sad mom.

Then a happy day,

rations of food,

hardly enough to fill our appetite,

but we have food.

Rotten, smelly meat,

vegetables full of bugs and insects,

rice with mice droppings,

but we do not have many choices to be picky.

My father makes the best fried, crispy fish,

served with rice in warm water.

My siblings and I sit in a circle,

salivating,

patiently watching Dad fry fish in oil.

Mom washes kale and tosses it in hot lard,

green mustard boiling violently with pork skin.

Everyone goes to bed with a satisfied stomach.

Day after day,

people are leaving for

America, Australia, France, Canada, Laos.

Mom cannot persuade Dad to go forward.

The bickering continues.

Despite their differences,

they still work hard to make sure we

do not go hungry.

Both of my parents are artists

in their own special way.

Before Dad gets his own jewelry shop,

he sets aside his pride,

and helps Mom

sew story cloths for

the Christian and Missionary Alliance (CAMA),

where American workers

sell Hmong crafts to foreigners.

They sew to fill the long hours of idleness,

uncertainty,

waiting.

After nearly five years of working day and night,

Dad saves enough money to

become a gold and silversmith,

opening his own jewelry shop.

Mom's brothers send money

from America to support their sister.

Mom sews every day and

promises to show me how to sew

soon.

Mai Lia: Grandma.

I receive cassette tape recording from

youngest brother Bee.

Hard believe

went America 10 years ago.

Bee,

kindest,

most thoughtful,

trusted brother,

said America beautiful country,

nothing like dirty, filthy place he left.

"Come, Sister,

I cannot bear to see you living in

this horrid condition.

Think of your children,

imagine their future;

do you want them to go back to a

life of poverty,

no education,

no future

like us?

Come, I sponsor your family."

His words inspire,

make me hopeful.

I harden heart,

decide no matter what husband say or

Mai Chao

rumors

about America,

I take children better place.

Rumors,

yes;

we know not what believe,

or sort what real anymore.

Now,

rumors funny;

back then,

nothing to compare,

no knowledge what true and not.

How foolish,

but rumors seem real.

Doctors and hospitals,

Hmong women wear no clothes,

hospitals like death house for elder people,

how frighten we feel.

How can we trust them?

Thankful,

I believe one person not fill my mind of lies.

Bee paint different picture of America.

Heart excited yet scared,

but know he right about children.

Rumors that refugee camps closing,

food and support going away like drying well.

Thai government and international relief agencies

not want burden of refugees in Thailand;

they want people out.

Refugee camps not meant permanent settlements.

Men talk go back

fight Communism.

Hmong men return Laos.

Money pooled together support lost cause,

freedom fighters.

I threaten Ginu not be involved,

or I leave.

Take children to America.

I not suffer in jungle,

let children see poverty,

same fate.

Pa Ying,

smart brain,

quick thinking,

good girl.

She help make money now by

sew story cloths.

Do you know story cloths only important after

Vietnam War?

Ancestors made flower cloths

or *paj ntaub*

as long as Hmong existed.

Paj ntaub,

women art of sewing,

stitch patterns and shapes

use have meanings,

connect Hmong to ancestors back China.

Meaning lost and change in

passing time,

war,

fleeing.

I remember each year in Laos,

brothers buy large roll fabric for mother and me.

We sit outside main door in evenings,

soak rays sunlight and sew paj ntaub,

happy together.

Evening light cast shades on ground,

birds sing night songs,

memories simple, joyful, childhood.

Our paj ntaub

stitch together to make

new clothes for family members at

New Year celebration.

Bad luck wearing last year's old clothes to celebration.

Mother and I spend hours after hard day work;

everyone get new clothes.

Story cloths come life in refugee camp to

pass time and tell story

what happen to Hmong.

We sew pictures show farming in mountains,

run from war,

live refugee camps,

come America.

Everything I learned about

paj ntaub Mother taught me.

I teach Pa Ying to sew,

be good daughter-in-law,

follow Hmong way of life.

I ask Ginu leave camp.

Maybe our five children have brighter future if leave.

I want children have more life.

I watch kerosene lamp show

dancing shadows around small room;

children sleep.

Each time see them,

promise in Laos come back.

Ginu work hours in jewelry shed with friends,

make silver earrings, necklaces, bracelets.

He best gold and silversmith in camp.

He happy man.

People come all over camp buy jewelry.

Once a week,

Ginu and friends take rest from work,

travel around selling

to women and young girls.

Tired,

he come sit by me on hard bamboo platform bed.

I nervous to talk about America, but do anyway.

"I wish follow brothers to Mis-con-sin.

Come with us?"

"We are not going anywhere,

disobedient Hmong woman!

We stay here and wait

to see what happens next," he says.

No stopping this time,

I determine go without husband.

"Nothing here for us.

You decide if want come or stay.

I take children with me;

you stay, not us.

Look around,

still waiting after 10 years. For what? For..."

Husband get furious, interrupts.

"You think you are such a smart woman?

Think again.

We are not going anywhere!"

he shout at me,

nostrils flare like water buffalo,

anger fill eyes.

"I decided.

We leave with or not with you."

Shock by strong words, Ginu storm out house.

I turn see children.

Pa Ying's eyes stare wide into mine.

"Go sleep, *me ntxhais*, my darling daughter."

Terrible dreams fill slumber,

dead people chase us in jungle,

pull me under water,

decay drip from skeletal bodies,

lost.

I scream and scream,

only find comfort sweet children

breath soft nearby.

I determine bring them America

at expense to lose husband,

be called bad daughter-in-law,

shame family reputation.

My children matter most.

Each year,

2,000 refugees leave camp.

Many die starvation,

diseases,

malaria,

tuberculosis.

Some commit suicide for

hopelessness and breaking hearts.

Thought of easy death

enter mind countless times;

I refuse be coward.

I fight hard and long stay alive,

I not die and leave children orphans.

Husband roam camp like

single man

without family.

All hopes and dreams are children.

Heart weeping

in

pain.

Ginu: Grandpa.

My love for Mai Lia has changed.

Who is she to challenge me,

her husband,

her owner?

I have no desire to go to America.

The demand for men is high in camp

since thousands

died during the war.

My friends are looking freely at

widows and young girls for multiple wives.

There is no harm in looking.

My dream is coming true,

and our jewelry shop is known

throughout Ban Vinai.

I am Ginu,

the silver and goldsmith,

wherever I go.

I am someone important.

Girls,

women,

give themselves to me for a

free pair of earrings or bracelets.

I feel valued,

respected,

admired,

wanted,

like a sought-after prize.

Let me tell you something, Kajsiab,

so you do not make this mistake, ever.

You must protect yourself

when you are old enough to do

husband duties.

Do you understand what I mean?

"Gross, Grandpa. I don't want to know."

You just wait, son.

I do not think I would

get sick from fooling around.

What have I done?

I no longer have the strength I used to have.

Weak,

uncomfortable,

and constant urination.

I should have stayed faithful to Mai Lia.

What if she leaves me behind with this

shameful disease?

You do not need to include this in your project,

but I want to make sure you understand

that there are many ugly things in life

that your Mom and Dad

cannot protect you from.

You must come to know many things on your own.

Family is everything.

I am lost without family.

For the first time in my life,

I may yield to Mai Lia's request,

only if she can help cure my illness,

only if she promises to stay with me,

even when I have been dishonest,

betrayed her trust.

She can learn to love me like she once did.

When I break the news of my infidelity,

she covers her face with her hands

and cries pitifully,

pouring furious tears into a sea of sadness.

For the first time in a long time,

I want to protect her,

but then,

I am a man.

I have no desire to show weakness,

frailty,

to a woman

who is inferior,

subordinate,

controllable.

"Help get me clean, and we can speak of America."

Being a good mother and wife,

she obediently helps me search

for Hmong herbs, advice, knowledge of curing this

sordid, disgusting disease.

One year of drinking bitter root concoctions,

bathing my lower body

three times a day

in rancid, brown liquid

Mai Lia boils for me,

staying away from troubled women,

I no longer feel itchy or uncomfortable.

Mai Lia smiles more each day as

I become cleaner.

The sun has set long ago with

streaks of red across the burning sky.

Thailand is terribly hot and humid in the evenings.

I lay in bed fanning myself piteously with

a paper fan.

Mai Lia joins me after washing her feet.

"I have decided to go to America with you," I say.

"I don't believe you," she says.

"Here is my proof to you.

Let's go tomorrow to the United Nation's office."

Talks of closing Ban Vinai become evident as

food rations decrease and

more Hmong are forced to go back to Laos.

You see, Kajsiab,

the Hmong people must split up once more,

even when we have nothing left.

A group of Hmong already

fled to Wat Tham Krabok,

a monastery,

to avoid repatriation.

I can no longer bear seeing Mai Lia's tears.

The sky is blue,

clear of clouds,

a good omen for our family to leave.

We enter the United Nation's office.

A tall White man in a clean white shirt

and a White woman with sun-kissed brown hair

look at us with stern, serious faces.

A young Hmong male translator sits nearby.

They shake our hands

and ask questions about

my involvement with Americans;

I proudly show them the compass

I used to guide my family from Laos to Thailand.

More questions about our family.

"Do you have more than one wife?"

"No, one is enough."

Everyone laughs.

My family passes the interview with ease.

I begin to panic as

we are about to embark on a

one-way journey,

no turning back.

We leave the UN office.

Too soon,

we are approved

to come to America.

Reality sets in

I feel unhappy,

depressed at the thought of leaving all I know.

My face hardens,

rigid and cracked like the dry earth

beneath my feet.

I am afraid,

and yet,

I must not show it to my wife or family.

I do not want to die in America,

oceans away from my homeland.

Three days before we are to leave,

Mai Lia and I argue because I refused to get ready.

My promise to her is dissolving before our eyes;

we shout terrible words and

fight like enemies.

The day before we leave,

I drag my crying wife to the United Nations office

to cancel our plans to go to America.

It seems everything is against me on this particular day.

The sky is gloomy,

threatening clouds of rain,

like a funeral procession heading to burial ground.

I wear a mask of disbelief and

fume with anger.

Out of the corner of my eyes,

I see Mai Lia plead to the somber sky.

I am a desperate man.

Dust swirls after our quick feet as

we race toward our destination.

Surprise, shock,

fury.

The building is dark,

closed.

My heart sinks, and I scream

sheer hatred

toward those invisible foreigners.

"You win. I'll come with you," I say.

Too numb to talk, she nods,

takes our children by their little hands,

heading home.

I sit on the steps until

I regain my sanity and composure.

Slowly,

I follow my family back to Center 7.

By morning the next day,

Ban Vinai is a memory of the past.

January, 1992:

On the bus ride,

I see fireflies glowing on

the Thai countryside.

I imagine each firefly to be like a dream,

blinking before my eyes.

Dreams disappear

but reappear,

tantalizing, enchanting,

like stars that shine.

I store their neon bursts of light in my memory.

Someday I will gather them,

tell my children that dreams are like fireflies;

they do not fade or disappear,

only glow brilliantly,

floating in a bottle,

like dreams in our hearts.

Phanat Nikhom Processing Center,

our new home for the next six months of

intense training and medical screening.

It is unlike anything I know,

strange,

like a baby learning to walk.

Chapter 7

Pa Ying: Mother.

"Mom, how much did you sell your first story cloth for?"

I smile with pride,

my sweet boy,

butterfly bathed in sunshine.

This National History Day project is

turning him into an investigator.

My baby is still searching for his fireflies.

In the meantime,

my fireflies

are wandering in this world.

"Well son, the Thai *baht* is like the American dollar.

My first story cloth shows many animals from Laos.

Hmong artists draw them on cloth as a way of preserving

these creatures in our minds.

I remember how I'd stitch every day

for an entire month

on my 12-inch,

navy blue,

square cloth.

I sit in the shade by my mother and

embroider with her girlfriends.

The women gossip about camp life,

news from abroad,

fears of leaving camp.

I sit with the women every afternoon to sew.

My neck is stiff, and my back aches

from bending long hours,

but I am cheerful to be

working side by side with my

mother.

Someday the discipline and effort in working hard

will help me

prepare for life.

After a month of sewing,

the embroidery is complete;

I stroll over the camp to sell my handiwork.

A Hmong lady from Center 3 buys it for

17 baht.

At this time,

the exchange currency is 34 baht to 1 US dollar.

My heart is proud,

filled with joy at my big accomplishment.

"Mom, you got ripped off," Kashia interjects.

Although I only earned fifty cents,

the amount is a fortune in Thai baht to

a 9-year-old.

I offer the money to Mom so she can buy more food.

She refuses to accept it,

says I should

save and use it wisely.

The first thing I buy with the money is

a dozen eggs for my family,

one for each member to have at our evening meal.

I remember feeling valuable,

like an adult,

contributing to our family,

assisting Mother

for the first time.

My younger brother receives a

sugar-covered Thai donut;

my best friend Va and I

each get a bag of crunchy crackers.

The rest of my money

goes back to purchase two unstitched story cloths

and more colors of floss threads.

I feel wonderful making money,

helping support my family.

Kashia,

you have no idea how lucky you are

to be born

in a free country.

Children go to school,

enjoy the luxury of public education,

make art.

Teachers plant seeds in your minds

that take you to many roads of opportunity

where you can become somebody if you

work hard.

Because of grandpa's jewelry shop and

grandma's sewing,

they can afford my small tuition.

My schooling is

a half day of learning arithmetic and reading

in Thai and Laotian.

Poor children run around all day,

waiting,

staring hungrily for the milk vans to come.

Yes, sweetened condensed milk.

We stand in long lines,

hoping

to get a cup of that refreshing,

unfamiliar,

sweet liquid.

My stomach grumbles in disapproval.

I'm too hungry to care,

until that cold milk splashes in my dry throat.

Later in the evening,

when the air is a little cooler,

I turn to the ground to make drawings.

My artistic skills begin to grow in Ban Vinai.

The day starts with hot, windy,

red dust, swirling like tornadoes,

blowing garbage into the air,

children chasing after plastic bags and flying papers.

I am among the children

chasing after large pieces of newspaper.

Higher and higher the paper floats.

I hop up on one leg

and snatch a piece mid-air.

I return home and

wait for evening to come.

Mom uses compressed coal and wood logs

to cook on the family hearth;

I sweep the ashes every morning before school.

I save small coal pieces and

little charred wood in a container

to draw on the ground when I return home.

I love the dark, black, bold lines

from these tools.

Stick people,

dogs and cats,

houses,

raindrops,

sun,

shapes.

Anything my mind conjures up,

I scratch onto the ground.

In a way I am subconsciously

recording a time,

a place,

and a group of people

through my art.

One day at school,

my Hmong teacher draws two beautiful parrots on

the black chalkboard.

The red and blue birds look like they could

fly out of that board

into this world.

He brings delight and pleasure

to our spirits that day.

His art is food for our hearts,

fulfilling,

rewarding,

a gift from the human soul.

I will remember my first experience when

art transcends words,

only emotions and feelings of joy,

inspiring,

powerful,

kindling my spirit into one with this universe,

my first encounter with a real artist.

From that day onward,

I draw whenever I can,

using the ground as my chalkboard.

Eventually,

my stick people have shapes,

forms, volume,

becoming more realistic.

Just as I am getting better at making accurate

drawings and recordings,

my parents decide it is time to pack up and

leave

Ban Vinai.

I remember the ground canvas drawings.

Etched into memory like grooves artists create with their tools,

childhood collections of thoughts

burn

like fireflies fading

into obscurity.

Mai Lia: Grandma.

America.

10,000 mile from Thailand,

night class,

full-time job,

I become adult child.

Leave hopeless and despair back,

like dying and reborn one more time.

"Grandma, did you have any idea of what

America might look like?"

Kajsiab come every few day

talk and ask question

for big Hmong project, he say.

Anger deep in heart for

daughter think know all.

Wish get over so I enjoy grandson.

I love him,

but foreign blood

cannot change.

"We hear scary story about America, Kajsiab.

Everything negative, not believable,

but we believe.

No place for us compare America but Laos,

Hard life of refugee camps in Thailand.

Let me tell you

Phanat Nikhom Processing Center,

last stop before settling new country."

Six month

learn survival English,

get educated about new country life.

When we cry last goodbye to

friends and family in Ban Vinai,

long green bus take us new camp,

Phanat Nikhom.

People leave,

go somewhere

everyday.

"We will meet again.

Don't lose hope," friends and relatives say.

Adults cry like children,

Reach hand out bus window

touch

one another last time.

Bus crawl out Vinai like caterpillars,

away from throngs people come say

goodbye

to loved ones.

Our bus full, majority Hmong,

some Cambodian, other refugees,

men, women, children,

throw up plastic bag,

body ache,

weak from motion sickness.

Not ride in car before,

unused to movement.

Rice paddies stretch both

sides black paved road.

Bus seats hot, sticky,

uncomfortable.

Ten then twelve hours,

losing track time.

We arrive morning,

foggy, chilly without warmth of sun yet,

find small city envelope

in grayness.

Long rectangular cement buildings,

three families to share one building.

White,

maybe pale blue,

dark gray

exterior,

tin roof pitter-patter like

bullets when rain come.

Two large blankets divide each family.

No privacy,

loud noise,

fear of thieves and assassins.

No door, but hole

empty space where door should be.

I remember electricity posts,

moths, bugs, night creatures

go to pretty light.

Everybody look for something

brighter in life.

Still,

life in Phanat Nikhom nicer.

Better living condition, food, clothing,

give us more human dignity and face.

I sew story cloths, but not often.

I go school now,

my first time ever in school,

almost 30 years old.

Rough farming fingers not know make

pen write words,

unlike needles I embroider easy.

I modest woman, but that

cannot stop me from

watching Thai movie at

1 baht movie house.

Hmong culture changing,

adapt Thai music, food, language,

especially young boys and girls.

Movie house,

big crowded room,

hard packed earth floor,

large screen TV,

young and old watch in wonder people fly,

no effort

like birds.

There I see first glimpse American.

They smile and laugh,

everyone happy.

I afraid sometime,

but I trust brother Bee.

I take children follow brother.

School.

I not set foot inside school before.

Only once I watch from window in Laos.

Father punish me not working fields that day;

I not go back.

How nice go learn read and write,

only mind no longer sharp,

tongue stiff as board.

We practice speak English during day,

attend Hmong writing class at night,

immunizations and medical exams

in between,

few hour sewing under kerosene lamp.

In camp I learn.

Hmong writing teacher in camp say

Hmong written language is young,

created by three kind hearts

love our people.

I forgotten names many time,

but now they stay in brain:

Dr. Linwood Barney,

Father Yves Bertrais,

Dr. William Smalley.

Handful smart Hmong friends

make script for our people,

get out middle age to modern time.

Hmong Romanized Popular Alphabet script,

1952.

Hmong RPA.

Great appreciation,

our words written down

to preserve language and culture,

we scatter over world

spreading, sharing, shifting.

Pa Ying come Hmong class to tutor.

She 9 years old.

Young mind like sponge,

remember,

understand thing I not remember long.

Someday she make me proud, I think.

Instead,

she turn against hopes and dreams of mother, father.

All sacrifice for nothing.

Children not listen,

not understand Hmong way.

I unhappy with choice.

Too much freedom for

girls

in America.

Ginu: Grandpa.

Patriarch,

decision maker,

powerful,

prestigious,

influential,

what I am accustomed to in Thailand and Laos.

America.

I am a nobody.

Starting our lives over at zero is

difficult and heartbreaking.

I struggle for control like a blind driver,

not knowing where we are heading,

what to encounter next,

or which path to take.

At times lost,

confused,

exasperated,

but at myself.

My education is limited;

farmers have no time for education.

Schools are out of reach for mountain dwellers.

In Laos,

I speak multiple languages

and know my land like the back of my hand.

In America,

I cannot help my children

with school work at home.

I expect them to get good grades,

have a strong work ethic

to compete with American students,

and carry on with Hmong values.

My duty

is to provide them with

food and shelter.

Their job is to go to school,

study hard,

become doctors or lawyers when they grow up.

They have secure futures

without worry or fear of not having enough.

Welfare system.

Refugee Cash Assistance.

Mai Lia and I both understand

we cannot survive on public assistance.

We are not afraid to work in this country.

We are given $1,000 from

the Refugee Cash Assistance program,

free clothing from generous church donations,

low income housing with numerous cockroaches,

to start our lives in America.

1992:

Life in America is unlike anything I have experienced.

Although the official documents say that I am 50 years old,

I am actually much younger.

My mother said that

I was born when the rice stalks were

young and tender.

She could not give me the exact year;

time was irrelevant,

as the mountain Hmong people

follow their own agricultural cycle based on

the monsoon and dry seasons.

It is in the refugee camps that

dates become important.

I make up birthdays for your grandma and me.

That is why many Hmong couples have the same birthdays,

only the year is different.

Easier to remember.

During most of the trip to America,

we do not talk much.

My children,

wide-eyed, watch, take in the

amazing sights and sounds of the new land.

I march in front with a serious mission to take everyone

safely to America,

navigating like I once did in the Mekong River,

witnessing the magic of the modern world before my eyes.

If we get lost,

I show the attendants at the airports

a piece of paper that says

we do not speak English

and are traveling to the United States.

That is how we find our way to America.

I remember getting off the plane at the airport,

seeing Mai Lia's brothers, relatives from my clan,

and new faces,

faces that we have

not seen in more than a decade,

mingling together with Americans.

We must be quite a sight,

wailing like children,

releasing the pain,

agony,

terror,

relief,

of this journey to a new world.

Of course,

some good Americans from the Catholic church come to

welcome us.

I remember Sheila's smile and teary eyes.

That kind woman.

She is one of the American organizers that help secure the

$1,000 refugee money,

food, clothing, and reduced housing for us.

Only she does not know that

family members can be

dishonest and crooked;

we start our lives in America with $200 for eight people.

Greedy Hmong relatives pocket most of the money

because we cannot read.

No matter,

we are through those days of relying on people

to hold our hands,

speak for us.

The years go by in the blink of an eye.

My first job is a janitor for a cleaning service.

I do not feel important anymore.

My children can read, write, translate now.

Thank you, teachers, for giving my children hope.

Immense gratitude to them for giving

my children a chance at life.

I only wish that my words were

not filtered down by

a child,

Pa Ying.

If only she were a boy,

I would be happier.

She has sharp,

quick-witted intelligence;

too bad she is a daughter, my first born.

Each year becomes harder for me to

watch my children

grow and take on American values.

We march at different rates of assimilation.

Assimilation?

More like surviving for me and Mai Lia in this country,

hanging on to every thread of Hmongness.

I am cautious,

slow,

and do not want to let go of the past.

Children.

Carefree,

light-hearted,

easily molded like melted wax.

I was once head of household,

supreme authority in my family;

no one dared question my decisions.

Each year, I lose more grip on my position,

my influence over our children,

especially my daughter,

Pa Ying,

who challenges everything I stand for.

What do these children in America know about

hard life and suffering?

We have suffered the pits of hell to survive,

yet,

children have no deep understanding of our sacrifices.

How dare they challenge and disobey their elders!

She is a mere girl,

fragile,

easily broken in the hands of men.

I have to protect her.

Strict curfews,

cook,

clean,

take care of brothers and sisters,

listen to her mother,

prepare to be a good housewife.

This nonsense of equality for women,

demanding her brothers

to help with chores after school,

speaking up at adult family meetings,

giving unwanted ideas and suggestions.

I refuse to admit in public

or to anyone that they are

clever and ingenious.

I refuse to acknowledge her intelligence.

Traditions forbid us to accept ideas from

simple-minded women who would make us

look and feel weak around them.

Pa Ying's mother does not complain

or question anything under my roof.

This is how life has been for women:

submissive,

inferior

to men.

I intend to keep this lifestyle as

we, Hmong men,

know it.

I see that schools are shaping our children,

turning them against

their own native tongue.

Pa Ying can read mail,

talk with authority figures,

translate anywhere.

I should be delighted.

Something inside me hates the idea of

this girl getting too much

respect and power.

She is undermining me as a man,

reducing my role, my status

as head of household.

I cannot bear to see her slick tongue

uttering English

at fifty miles an hour.

Her haughtiness,

arrogance,

thinks she can do anything she wants,

like a man.

We demand her to be traditional,

follow our old ways of life,

be an obedient Hmong daughter,

bring honor and grace to our reputation.

Instead,

she plays sports

and grows large muscles,

which will affect her ability to bear children.

Mai Lia and I are exchanging nasty words

more each day,

about our children.

She has no control over her rebellious daughter.

I fear losing her to this invisible monster,

America.

It threatens to steal the ethos

and language of our culture

as beliefs change.

2002:

A decade passes by

like wind

finding shelter

on a rocky shore.

My heart still yearns for home.

Mai Lia and I work opposite shifts so

I can take classes

at the technical college in the morning;

she takes care of the children in the afternoon.

Ten years of working toward my education,

I earn my General Education Diploma.

Ten years of perplexity

asking for help on homework.

Pa Ying used to do assignments for me,

until she got smarter,

refusing to do them.

She reads the directions,

shows me how to solve the problems,

drops hints,

but I am too tired and old to think.

She should just do them for me;

I get good grades when she does the assignments.

I brought her here to study and learn;

the least she can do for me is my work.

She is just a daughter;

someday she will leave my family to

benefit a new one.

What do I get out of this?

A few thousand dollars of dowry money for

years of feeding and clothing her.

Over 10 years,

I pay $25 every month for

our plane tickets to America.

Do any of my children know about this?

Of course not.

Except for Pa Ying,

who writes out the checks.

Everyone else is too busy becoming

Americanized.

I am a disappointed father.

I just want to close my dark and anxious eyes,

return to a place

that fills my heart with singing crickets,

rejoicing in the green carpet of wavy hills and mountains.

Chapter 8

Pa Ying: Mother.

I remember my "firsts" in America.

Seeing the magic of snowflakes

dancing like white feathers in the air,

tasting the cold sky fruit with my tongue,

drinking boiling brown liquid after ice skating,

being very happy

doing American things.

My favorite part of the year is Christmas time.

Presents given to us by caring strangers,

thoughtful and kind,

making sure we are not left out

or

forgotten.

Aside from the gifts,

I love the spirit of the American people.

Beautiful lights hanging in a clean city,

giving hearts,

being together with families,

celebrating life.

Soft curves of snow covering everything in

a blanket of whiteness.

My life perpetually shaped by caring teachers,

thoughtful friends at school.

I begin to see the world through

my "American" eyes

the day Mrs. Whitely's dog dies.

Sad,

tragic

a new beginning for her,

an eye-opening event for me.

1992:

My first American teacher,

curly brown hair,

wears jeans every day.

Only wealthy people in Ban Vinai

can afford jeans or "cowboy" pants,

so I instantly think:

Mrs. Whitely is rich.

She has a wonderful smile;

her voice reminds me of

wind chimes gently playing music in the wind.

Through her gentleness and patience,

I am able to understand her.

This particular day,

her eyes are red and puffy

like the eyes I have seen on my mother.

She tells the class that her dog was sick;

they put him to sleep last night,

and now she misses him.

What?

Why sad when her dog is only sleeping?

Surely he will wake up again.

She is in tears,

mourning,

lamenting her grief.

It died?

How odd to cry for an animal as if it were a person?

American children

crowd around the teacher's desk to hug

and comfort her,

while the Hmong kids

stand respectfully nearby.

My best friend Va translates the situation.

In Ban Vinai,

dogs and cats are a nuisance,

wild and unwanted,

dirty and loitering

near people like scattered garbage.

No one looks or pays attention to

these filthy animals.

For the first time,

I realize that animals are special in America,

like friends and family members for people.

Through Mrs. Whitely's sadness,

I begin to see and feel the world with new eyes.

That is when I first notice my heart is

in love

with a new culture.

By fifth grade,

my second year in America,

1993:

I know deep in my heart that

going to school and getting good grades

is my only ticket to freedom,

to a better life,

to help lift my family out of poverty,

while paving a new path for

future generations.

I have high hopes, big dreams.

I want to have wings and fly.

I refuse to let someone define my role as

a housewife

when I grow up.

I want more in life.

Who wants to get married anyways?

My parents are not good role models

when it comes to marriage.

All I see is anger and frustration,

putting each other down

to score cheap points in front of other people.

Quarreling

over money,

over how terrible the other is raising the children,

over just about anything

whenever the two are together.

Like gasoline and fire,

they are not friends,

have fallen out of love,

and are only staying together

for the sake of their children.

I seldom see them happy together, ever.

Mom,

culturally bound to traditions,

stays with Dad

no matter how heartbroken,

miserable,

her life is.

She is committed to him.

I cannot bear to see her sadness,

helplessness,

getting walked over like a dirty rug.

She works hard to keep the family together,

without once complaining about her tough life to anyone,

not even to her brothers who could help speak to him.

Three years after we arrive in America,

1995,

I vow to not put myself in that position to a man.

Secretly,

I am determined to create my own life,

take my own unbeaten path,

pray that I am not forced to marry too soon.

School is the only place I feel safe,

free to think,

valued as a person,

not wasting my time

cleaning,

cooking,

looking after someone else.

I am like a second mother at home,

taking care of the household

when both parents must work.

I do not mind,

but I am growing up too fast.

Domestic violence

happens in every culture.

I have seen father's angry,

twisted face

of hatred

hitting mother during fights.

"You bad wife!

Dead face woman!

Don't know why I married you!"

He forgets that

she was forced into this relationship.

Her bruised body,

soft, thin whisper,

tearful around her children,

forcing herself to

not share her dreary life with anyone,

hanging on to a thread of hope that

some day

her children

make it worth

the pain and suffering.

I get older and see more of his abuses.

Horrified,

scared,

I step in front to take some blows.

Father stops hitting and pushes me aside.

"Do you want to die too?"

he screams and leaves the house.

Slowly,

the abuse stops because he does not want to go to jail.

Teachers might see my bruises and come after him.

He knows several men have been jailed

for hitting their kids.

Mom and I share a special bond,

unspoken;

we both want to fly away from

our daughter cages.

"How does it feel to read and write?

Maybe someday you become doctor?" she asks with pride.

I begin teaching her what I learn in school.

She is tired in the evening,

so our lessons dwindle down.

I promise to do my best in school.

Violence in the Hmong community

often goes unreported until it is too late.

My good friend Jimmy

loses both parents in one day.

Jimmy was born in America, and

his parents proudly

named him after

the most powerful man at the time,

President Jimmy Carter.

They hope his namesake will bring

good luck and prosperity

to the family.

He and I love to play basketball and soccer

together during recess,

but after school,

Jimmy belongs to a Hmong gang.

He feels protected,

valued,

respected with his friends.

The fighting between his parents starts on

a Friday night

in a two-story apartment:

the stress of work,

tangled disappointment in children,

hard life of making ends meet,

struggle with roles and identity,

changes in this new land.

Out of defeat,

Jimmy's father tells his seven children to go upstairs

so the adults can talk downstairs.

He locks all doors,

blasts the stereo

so no one can hear them,

takes out his shotgun

and kills his wife,

then shoots himself

while his children wait upstairs.

Jimmy knows what gunshots sound like;

he becomes suspicious.

He calls his relatives first then tries to

come downstairs.

The door by the stairs is locked;

the three oldest children kick the door

and free themselves to see

the grotesque scene of their parents death.

The children are divided,

sent to live with different relatives around the state.

I have not seen my friend again.

I still think of Jimmy and his family

when I go by that part of town.

His mother was my mom's friend.

My mother is brave,

courageous,

protective.

She is a vigorous woman

like the lone cypress tree

in Pebble Beach, California:

over 200 years old,

iconic,

enduring years of beating from elements,

a testament of beauty and time.

I do not want to disappoint her.

Mai Lia: Grandma.

This world wide, endless.

Furtherest saw in Laos next valley.

America bright, beautiful, tall building.

Many car, road, light, pretty home.

New sight, sound, smell.

How can ghosts roam in big city?

Maybe they stay in Laos and cannot

cross Mekong River.

I think our dead people time to time,

heart cry for dear mother and father,

wish they see nice city, Mis-con-sin.

Not know how help children in America

I say do best in school I cook for them.

School their job;

my job work, cook, feed them at home.

Work different in America,

use brain to think,

less labor with body,

I work for sewing company

make tuxedos.

I cannot read or write good,

but I fast learner,

not afraid try speak American

or make mistake.

American lady show how sew, and I copy.

My sewing pretty, fast, quick learner.

Boss happy man.

No complain.

Grateful to work

bring money home,

feed children.

Life in America great,

wish husband understanding,

but hard change old man,

"qub neeg qub siab"

same person,

same liver,

never change.

Ginu that way since children come.

No love,

fight,

and fight,

upset all time with me.

He change,

unhappy with life,

take frustration on wife

because he want power,

break me down to feel strong man.

Like actor fly from 1 baht movie house,

wish I travel back time,

not leave mother and father,

see wind ripple through rice and corn fields,

hear bird sing,

heart light with little worry.

I alright now that children go school,

learn, get smart,

hopeful.

I glad see them here

instead

Laos,

no future.

Pa Ying smart girl,

good brain,

remember and understand fast.

We not like her play sports,

run everyday,

come home late.

She a girl not a boy.

People talk.

She not listen and join anyway.

I losing control over daughter.

Too much freedom,

Feel little respect for elder.

Ginu and I not like it.

We fight her day and night.

1999:

Now she in high school and drive.

Hmong men come; she hide in room.

Disrespectful, but no blame daughter.

She like school and want marriage wait.

Two marriage proposal,

no choice

we tell family wait.

Pa Ying finish school first, then marry.

Daughter almost done high school;

few Hmong boys visit home.

Not good.

Do not know why she picky.

I two babies when her age.

Older men come to house during weekend,

but she not home;

at library or

go with American girl play sport.

Ginu furious,

raging violent words that

cut wounds in heart.

Blames me.

Want me control daughter and

force obey.

She big girl and not listen.

No trouble at school,

good grades,

only stubborn,

rebellious,

quick mouth.

All the time,

I see her read and draw.

My other children different.

Watch television,

no open book.

She not talk

to me or Ginu,

go bedroom,

homework,

draw,

out for snack,

help brother and sister homework,

off to bed.

I worry.

I hear rumor blow around like leaves

she has boyfriend.

Not Hmong.

A White boy

I afraid

to meet.

Ginu: Grandpa.

The sky seems hardly blue,

even if there are no clouds.

Sun glinting off rooftops and windows,

making it difficult for my eyes to see.

I am sightless

and insignificant.

My heart is unsettled like turbulent rapids

cutting through rock.

My skills from Thailand are

useless here.

I feel small

like an ant

drowning in this strange society.

After several years of this dead-end work,

I join Glod'n Plump,

where we butcher chickens

in a large, lonely warehouse.

I tolerate a few years

and cannot endure the

sights and sounds of death

in that warehouse.

It reminds me too much of the war

and the old life we left.

If I tell you how we killed those chickens,

I guarantee you will become a vegetarian.

Someone has to do the dirty job

to bring meat to the markets.

For the last fifteen years,

I worked for the same company as

an assembly line worker.

My wage started at $4.45 an hour;

I am making $12.00 now.

We make parts that go in cars like buttons and knobs.

This is where I meet and interact with Americans.

We do not understand their culture and language well,

so we smile to show our friendliness.

They take that as a sign of

weakness and stupidity.

Some are rude to us.

Let me tell you something about

those Americans;

they are different from our people.

Their harsh tones, jeering eyes,

pointing their fat fingers with hatred

in our faces as if

we are idiots

when we work together on

the assembly lines.

Yes,

there are some friendly Americans that work there,

treat us with respect and dignity,

but they stay away.

At lunch,

all the Hmong eat together,

all the Mexicans eat by themselves,

all the White people scatter around

or sit in little groups.

We have not had

many positive experiences

with Americans.

I forbid my children

to dye their beautiful black hair

yellow or blonde

like those little gangsters around here.

Hair is a symbol of beauty and prosperity

in a woman.

That is why your mother has long hair.

When I hear the news of your mother dating your father, Kajsiab,

I become furious

that the only thing I think of is a deep,

violent rage inside.

I do not know if I should be honest and frank with you.

"My feelings won't be hurt.

I want to know our family story, Grandpa."

I think to myself,

I should have left her to die in Thailand.

She betrayed her parents,

forgot all the dangers,

hardships,

and sacrifices

your grandma and I made

to bring her here.

In the end,

this is what we get:

betrayal,

disappointment,

and loss of hope.

How can I face my clan?

I am the first one to have

a humiliating daughter.

My position as head of household is compromised,

questioned by the people who

value and respect

my authority.

If I cannot even make my own daughter obey,

then why should other people listen to me?

I burn incense sticks to our ancestors and

ask for a miracle to happen.

Pa Ying,

get over this White guy and find a decent

Hmong man to marry.

Hmong and American people do not belong together.

How can she love a man who looks nothing like her?

I am sickened.

If we still lived in Laos,

this would not happen in our family.

I cannot allow my own daughter to disobey me.

She must do as I say;

my words are the law.

End of story.

Not here.

In America children fight back,

make us look like evil parents.

The story goes on whether I like it or not.

2002:

She is in her first year of college,

shrewd girl,

lives at the University and

only comes home on weekends.

That is another battle I lost to her.

We demand that she comes home every night,

but she claims to need the quiet space, her privacy to study.

I hope she tells the truth

and not spend every minute with him.

I am distressed each day, as if my mind is full of

hornets.

Mai Lia and I invest money

paying shamans to cast spells,

performing spiritual healing ceremonies on Pa Ying,

with no success.

Our spiritual healers have successful outcomes;

we just have a bullheaded,

stubborn daughter

possessed by a White demon.

The only time I feel content is during the summer.

I can work in the cucumber fields

with friends and family members

like the old days in Laos.

We work every hour of the day

from sunrise to sunset.

I feel a sense of accomplishment knowing that

my two bare hands

have done something special with the earth,

which generously feeds my family.

Each summer we grow two acres of cucumber plants,

hand-picked,

and sell them to a

rich White farmer called Pat.

He turns around and sells them to big pickle companies.

The work is hard like farming in Laos,

but I feel connected to the land,

the living earth that creates life from the soil.

I miss the simple days of work that

feeds my family

year after year.

Pa Ying: Mother.

I meet Josh

in my Advanced Placement government class

during my junior year.

My first impression of him is,

'Wow, what a big head!'

I laugh

and think of Beavis and Butthead.

There is something about him that makes me feel

at ease.

I can be my true self around him.

My shyness disappears as I let him see my world.

I sit across from him

and love to draw his face

in a variety of artistic styles,

from caricature to manga to realistic rendering.

I like the way his eyes shine

with kindness,

a calm smile;

his face still makes me laugh.

This is the beginning of my life where

it starts to matter.

I am the only Hmong student in

many AP classes,

and often I feel stuck between two crowds.

Josh is pleasant around the Hmong kids because

he loves to play soccer with them.

One day,

he invites me to join his study group.

Soon we become study partners for

the AP test.

We study vigorously in the school library.

Each time we meet,

he brings a stuffed animal pal to study with us.

I love his carefree spirit.

He has stirred feelings deep inside my heart,

like igniting a flame, but

I cannot put a finger on my emotions.

The only thing I know for sure is that

my heart beats faster when we are close.

I have guarded it to avoid

getting hurt.

Josh is disarming my walls with this

newness of longing

to have him in my universe.

Love makes me feel like

I can reach the sun

or touch the moon,

unlike my mother,

who feels like a caged animal.

The sweet taste of honey,

melting my soul into a puddle of

warm delight.

We become friends and feel the

electricity of love

passing between us.

Laughing, joking,

not a worry on my mind

each time I see him.

Our skin colors disappear,

our cultures fade into the background;

we are just two teenagers connecting.

He scores a perfect five on his AP test.

I am proud of my three.

I feel part of America now.

Breathtaking bluffs remind me vaguely of

the mountains

my parents left long ago.

Each time I go up the roads leading to

the scenic overlook

of the calm city,

I see how far our people have come.

This splendid landscape is

their new home.

What are their hopes and dreams?

I must not forget the hardships and sacrifice

my parents go through each day

so I can learn,

become somebody if I work hard,

believe.

They do not see it the way I do.

Each side refuses to see the other.

I know that getting an education is

my only ticket to a freer life.

Josh and I continue to be friends until

the end of the year.

Summer

comes like a breeze

through an open window.

The two marriage proposals

no longer threaten

my freedom;

the men cannot wait any more

and find themselves

petite wives from Laos.

Thank the heavens!

Father still pressures me

to date and get married,

so he can gain face and

pride

by having a son-in-law.

I tell him I want to get my college degree first;

then I will be ready to settle down.

"Daughter, you will be an old maid.

Who wants to marry a woman with a college degree?"

"I can be a happy old maid,

living with you and Mom forever then," I say.

"Your mother was younger than you when I married her;

you need to prepare to be a good housewife.

Do not bury yourself in books and drawings

all the time.

They will not make you a useful wife to a man."

Father seldom talks to me,

except when he is giving advice or

needs my brain to work for him.

I am insulted by his words but hold

my tongue rigid

out of respect.

"You cannot go to college to be an artist.

It is a low-paid profession with

little prestige and honor.

I recommend you become a doctor or a lawyer."

Here goes his contradiction,

wanting me to be successful,

at the expense of tying myself down to a man.

I hear this speech often.

"Find a husband who can help you with your schooling

while you are still young."

I can handle my own schooling.

They do not understand me.

Maybe I do not understand them,

two wavelengths traveling at different speeds.

I stop talking about

my dreams

at home.

Giving up drawing and reading for a few days

is unbearable;

my soul cannot escape reality,

craving intellectual food to fuel my mind.

Books are like the constellations in the sky,

open,

free,

endless.

My world is incomplete,

trapped in a stifling culture,

like a captured firefly

inside a glass jar.

People are more self-centered

than what my parents are accustomed to.

The only thing constant is change.

We must adjust with time

or perish like dinosaurs.

Living in America is like

playing tug-of-war every day.

They want me to be successful in

American society

in order to help them,

but at the same time,

they want to trap me in

traditional roles.

Happiness,

for some people,

is about being successful.

That success to my parents

is wealth, because they have limited opportunities.

Not in love.

They refuse to recognize my artistic talent

and assume they know that

I would like to become a doctor or lawyer

because they make a lot of money.

They do not know

that their daughter is smart,

quiet,

and shy.

Mom and Dad also have no clue

how difficult it is to get into

medical or law school.

They are setting me up for

failure and disappointment.

I have other plans for my future.

Confusing,

that barrier of glass,

the Hmong in me,

catching glimpses of my American dreams,

hopes,

aspirations,

through a clouded jar.

Often I have one foot inside my Hmong home

while my other foot is stuck outside

my American environment.

I hate the summers when we do not have school.

My brothers,

boys,

can go where they want,

have no curfews,

independence.

Girls,

bound to the house,

not an inch of freedom

to experience this world.

No wonder

many Hmong girls get married at a young age,

hoping they will gain more independence

in their married lives,

only to find out that life is

even more demanding for them.

Parents are fearful that if

they give us a taste of freedom,

then we will misbehave,

get pregnant,

do drugs,

fly away.

Only negative thoughts enter their minds.

Do they ever stop to think that

if they teach their sons to behave properly,

perhaps they do not have to be

terrified for their daughters?

I am a proud Hmong daughter,

raised with good values,

but lately,

all the inequalities within my home

remind me that there is

much work to be done in our culture.

I once read a book about

Mahatma Gandhi,

Indian leader who brought his people together

through peace and non-violent actions.

His wisdom is inspiring.

"You must be the change you wish to see in the world."

Nothing will change unless

I alter my circumstances,

even when it is not popular,

even when I may have to stand alone.

Mai Chao

Father requests me to go wash dishes on purpose

as I do homework.

His sons sit and watch television.

It is not the work that infuriates me

but the idea,

the principle

behind his action that

I am inferior,

not as valuable as his sons.

Many Hmong households treat

their daughters the same way,

preparing them to be housewives

while their sons enjoy their license of being

proud boys,

pillars of society,

leaders of tomorrow.

Some go on to be successful and

feel responsible

for the direction of the Hmong people.

They practice what they preach,

living by a code of ethics that define who they are.

Ironically,

some of them are the ones Hmong people shun,

even feared.

I am eager to go to college,

explore this world and be at liberty,

contribute to something bigger,

bring honor,

respect,

and dignity to our family.

Being a daughter will not stop me

from following my dreams.

The day is bright.

Men twice our age come to find wives

in our neighborhood.

Wisely, we call each other before

they enter our apartments.

Two men knock on our door.

I dash to my bedroom,

refusing to come out.

Thank goodness for

my smooth-talking mother.

I hear her

giggling,

talking merrily with them.

Father would be infuriated if he were home

to witness my rudeness,

seeing his wife

chatting with other men.

Father locks her inside an invisible box

where she is not allowed to speak to other men,

and obligates her to bow down to his every wish.

I feel genuinely sorry for my mother,

who is not the only woman suffering.

Thousands of wives have no opportunity

or education

to improve

their standard of living or way of life.

America has opened my eyes,

emboldened my spirit,

helped me experience a life without

poverty and imprisonment.

Coming to America,

my mother's gift to her children.

For all that,

I can no longer bear to see

her tears of

helplessness,

loneliness,

isolation.

I have dreams.

Remembering how inspired I was when

I saw my first real artist,

I record stories

through my artwork.

Senior year, 2001:

Josh and I have different classes and

only see each other through passing.

I am a girl who likes to be close to home.

As much as I want to get away,

my home is where my family lives.

I do not have the courage to go to

the Chicago Art Institute.

They accept me,

but

I have a duty to stay close to home,

helping my parents.

Fall, 2002:

Autumn leaves drop lazily,

graceful to their end,

change of season.

Josh attends the same college as me.

One day,

by fate,

we see each other and start to talk.

My heart skips a beat at his quiet voice.

Suddenly with clarity,

his face no longer makes me laugh;

I notice his light brown eyes,

handsome face shining with kindness,

sweet laugh like wind bristling through leaves,

and, oh, his gentleness with words!

So different from any boy I know,

the opposite of my father.

Absolutely boyfriend material.

We exchange phone numbers and

promise

to play tennis soon.

In no time,

Josh and I are inseparable

like old friends.

His touch is delicate,

sincere.

He is the very air I breathe,

my oxygen,

the stars that twinkle.

His kisses send ferocious flames deep into my soul,

as if saying no one can break us apart;

I am yours.

Somehow I just know that

we are meant to love each other.

I am saturated by his glorious love.

Life seems brighter,

sweeter,

more alive.

Our relationship

blossoms,

flourishes

into something of our own.

Hope.

Butterflies flutter with joy in my belly.

There is no beginning,

no end,

no rules,

just the two of us

falling in love as two people do.

We come from different upbringings and cultures

yet,

have similar values

and share the same dreams:

to live an honest,

fulfilling,

happy life.

Accepting each other for who we are,

rather than Hmong woman and White man.

Love transcends skin color

when two hearts

come together

to beat as one.

Love

gives me

hope.

Josh: Father.

August, 2000:

Pa Ying sneaks into my heart like sunlight,

unbroken by clouds,

spreading happiness into

every corner of my world.

Her free spirit,

innocence of youth,

effervescent eyes

intrigue me.

She is the first woman that

I can imagine spending the rest of my life

growing old,

watching our children run,

shrieking in delight and laughter.

I have fallen in love with the idea of being in love,

but this time I feel its full intensity

like a tornado

sweeping across the plains of my heart.

Unrelenting,

the thought of her makes me ache,

vulnerable,

instinctual,

as if we have always known each other.

Being in love makes me feel

everything is possible.

I cannot wipe this smile off my face.

With no hesitation and remorse,

I give my heart to her.

We do not venture often out in public.

She insists we stay inside

until she is ready to face her parents,

her culture,

her people.

I am an American man with

Norwegian and German heritage.

I fall in love with Pa Ying first and then

her culture and family.

In the afternoons when Pa Ying comes to visit,

I hold her tight in my arms,

not wanting to let go,

afraid she may not come back to me.

Side by side,

we slow dance to Babyface crooning,

"Every time I close my eyes

I thank the Lord that I've got you..."

Three months go by in the blink of an eye.

Pa Ying and I build a web of trust and security

through honesty,

acceptance,

and friendship.

I would do anything for her.

Our relationship feels right;

we are made for one another.

Then her parents find out.

Insults and lectures begin.

They torment and terrorize her

every waking moment

as if our love is a thorn

they cannot remove from their hands.

My loving girl

endures the pain and misery day and night.

It is unbelievable how I can feel love and

hatred

at the same time,

an intangible,

ugly shadow

that buries itself within the walls of my heart.

Tunnel vision.

Narrow mindedness.

They are victims to ignorant fear.

Prejudice,

a vicious demon who

tears people apart,

consumes them with loathing.

Unable to understand

what it feels like to love someone beyond skin color,

Pa Ying's parents refuse to accept our relationship because

I am White.

They do not even know me and already

assume the worst.

In a way,

they are protecting their child.

"He will not love you long.

White and Hmong people

cannot live together.

We eat rice, and they eat bread.

He will leave you after he is through with you."

I am nothing like that.

Pa Ying comes to visit and stands still,

unsure of what to do or say.

Distraught, uncomfortable silence,

so many words lay on the tip of her tongue,

but none of them matter.

Some things are better left unsaid

because repeating only hurts more.

Tears roll down her cheeks.

As I gently kiss the salty drops,

I whisper into her ears,

"You are my life;

I'll take good care of you,

my love."

I promise.

"Thank you. You mean the world to me."

I speak gentle words,

coaxing her to smile, but

I see that tormented look in her eyes.

"Choose us or choose him.

Remember, we gave you life.

You would have died in Thailand

if it was not for us.

Maybe we should have left you

to die there.

You are making the biggest mistake of your life.

Leave him or else!"

I wish I could move the stars and the sun so

she does not leave.

She lays curled up beside me as

I smooth her lustrous black hair.

I just want her to be happy.

I am attracted to her beauty,

grace,

kindness,

silent iron strength.

Every time she leaves me,

she puts on a suit of armor

to fight for our love.

When she is with me,

fears,

worries,

doubts

are replaced by my undying love.

From the depths of my soul, I know

we would have found

each other sooner or later.

Inseparable,

I will not let go.

I fell in love with a girl.

It just happens that

she is from another culture.

The music of our love and

devotion

pumps through our veins,

the nourishing water of life.

We create this beautiful relationship

that some people can never understand.

The words they say are distasteful,

untrue, and

driven by guilt.

They live in the past,

both feet stuck deep in ancient mud,

unable to step away or move

forward.

They are her past, and

I am her future.

Hand in hand,

we write our own stories and build our own lives.

Strict cultural rules and obligations

do not intimidate me;

I cannot bear to see her shed tears.

We will find ways to honor her heritage.

For three years,

my love and I

ride this roller coaster of life as one.

I am ready to make her my wife.

I wish that she did not have to

choose between

her family

and me.

In the end,

I am grateful.

Through her art,

she is able to cope and find solace in

her painful decisions.

The sweetness of love

is tinged with sadness.

Bittersweet.

She does not have to doubt my love

because it is unconditional, pure and true.

Unlike her parents,

Pa Ying does not have to worry about

losing me;

I give myself freely,

peacefully to her,

and know deep down

that this girl loves me too.

Nothing in life has come easy for

Pa Ying or her people.

They work hard and fight

audaciously wherever they go.

Behind all the nasty, harsh words,

hide

two worried parents.

America has been kind to their children

by giving them boundless opportunities

to find their dreams and have a better life

that Mai Lia and Ginu can only imagine.

June, 2003:

We consulted our wonderful Hmong friend

and his beautiful Norwegian wife about marriage.

Their love, faith, and blessing gave us strength to

continue on with our journey.

Sunny and warm,

a slight breeze combs through our hair.

Pa Ying and I enter her parents' house.

Reality is inescapable.

I am sure of what

I must do.

My heart is pounding thunderously

while my mind spins like a whirligig.

By the time we leave this house,

anyone listening will know that

I love this girl.

My hand lacing tight with hers.

"Ready, darling?"

She nods and squeezes my hand tighter.

I am not afraid for myself but

worried for Pa Ying.

I appreciate that she translates for me,

even when it breaks her heart into pieces.

I have seen enraged faces and pointing fingers

waving in the air directed at Pa Ying.

Her relatives do not want me to understand or

hear their ugly words.

Pa Ying and I sit on a couch

as men sit on chairs surrounding us.

The women are in the kitchen,

listening,

waiting,

anticipating.

The house fills with elders from Ginu's clan.

Male voices dominate.

The air is electric, tense, pervasive.

After her parent's initial horror and shock,

it is clear that I am serious about

my marriage proposal.

This time,

I witness the aching tears,

pleading words from her family.

Pa Ying is reduced to a whisper,

her confidence disappearing

as she tries to bury herself by my shoulders.

Eyes cast down,

I see turmoil churning inside a young girl,

torn between family loyalty and

pursuing her dreams.

In that instant,

I know in my heart

she is my firefly,

a dream coming true before my eyes.

My voice becomes louder, clearer.

I have to be strong for us.

"This is not a game.

Are you serious

about marrying our daughter?" asks an uncle.

"Yes, I am serious.

I am fortunate to have found Pa Ying

and will love her no matter what."

Uncle translates our exchange.

I can sense the nervous energy

permeating the crowded living room

like a storm about to hit.

Questions and concerns,

the elders continue to throw at me

until two hours later

when they feel satisfied with my answers.

Slowly,

I begin to see the fire come back in Pa Ying's glistening eyes.

Women in the kitchen

wipe their tears of joy at how lucky she is

to find a man

who loves her.

They wish their husbands would be more like that.

Some think Pa Ying has just made

a grave mistake,

while others are glad that she may

avoid a life of privation and destitution.

Secretly,

the women envy her courage and determination.

Pa Ying's mother is sobbing,

but from joy, grief or sadness,

I cannot tell.

I can see relief and happiness

radiating from Pa Ying's face

like sunshine washing over me.

My eyes shine with love and gratitude.

She did not give up on us.

Big risks come with huge rewards.

I whisper to her,

"I love you."

At last, we are going to be together.

Like two fireflies

dancing in the night,

I am a happy man.

Chapter 9

Kashia: Son.

Each year

my dad takes me to see the Harlem Globetrotters

when they come to town.

I love their awesome ball handling skills and

silliness that make me laugh until my belly aches.

Basketball, my favorite.

My all time favorite baller is Michael Jordan,

mid 1980s - late 1990s,

shooting guard,

#23,

Chicago Bulls.

Watching MJ play is seeing a

powerful,

creative,

genius.

He wants to win every game,

plays his hardest each time.

This brilliant athlete inspires me to keep

working hard,

believing,

doing the best that I can.

Thinking about my National History Day project,

I have a pretty good idea of what I want to do now.

I need to be a voice for the Hmong people,

to make sure they are

not forgotten

in the American history books,

to give them the proper credit they deserve

as they make America

their new home.

Mai Lia: Grandma.

Three year shame,

waiting,

hoping Pa Ying and Josh not like each other.

When I go help family gathering,

I hear people gossip,

whisper,

talk poor about

bad daughter.

"How can you allow such disgrace in your family?"

"If I were you,

I would just force her to marry a Hmong man."

"Too bad we are in America;

otherwise you could still

protect your face and reputation."

"I give her two or three years with that White man;

he will grow tired of her."

I have mad heart.

No matter we say to Pa Ying about American,

she deaf ear.

Nothing,

nothing,

nothing change her mind!

She blind in love;

I fear future.

Not be angry what I say next.

Not want Pa Ying come back as

broken daughter;

no man want her rest life.

Loss face,

bad reputation

important to Hmong people.

We not want

half White children yellow hair

come back home.

Bad luck.

No matter what we say,

she choose White man over family.

Shame her.

She risk everything.

All done for her

down toilet

for White man.

Forget mother hard work,

give best part chicken before eat,

boil water wash her,

buy new clothes for her,

I wear old rags.

She forget Mother.

When she home from college,

I say nothing good.

I scream,

mad not care what come out,

spit poison word like dagger

inflict wound disgraceful daughter.

Most time I repeat

I hear people say,

hope this change her.

Ginu join shouting,

his word roar thunder,

sometime,

kick Pa Ying's door frustration.

She embarrassment,

family shame,

no longer

daughter.

Head get angrier as heart grow cold

I ask why we bring children here.

In return,

she abandon culture,

family,

mother and father.

In end,

I let go,

one at time

release lantern bug to nature.

From afar,

watch glow

and become

new people.

I try be satisfy

I did best bring them here for new life.

Nothing I can do, but cry

until

heart feel

empty.

Ginu: Grandpa.

Hmong people are accustomed

to working like a yoke of oxen with

their clans.

We are more powerful as one unit.

Try to break a handful of sticks.

It is harder to break a handful

compared to a single stick.

Snap!

Family is what I love about Hmong culture.

Do not forget where you come from.

I am sad that

our children are changing,

becoming Americans in their minds,

their needs,

their wants,

their dreams.

Individual, separate, single.

What about family?

What about us?

Brave people put families before

pride and needs.

Pa Ying is stepping on slippery stones.

Now,

I have six children growing up in America.

She is my only one to

attend a university.

I silently praise her for being brave,

but I do not agree with her choices,

nor do I approve her decisions

as if she does not need us anymore.

I have seen many Hmong girls

lost to this thing called

freedom,

only to return home,

begging for a place to stay.

Three years of unrest for Mai Lia and me.

We are self-conscious when we go out;

people want to give us advice

and express their opinions on

our unfortunate situation.

Three years of yelling,

until one day something I dread happens.

June, 2003:

I almost fall to the ground when

Pa Ying and Josh enter my house,

holding hands,

asking for permission

to be husband and wife.

Shocking,

audacious,

unthinkable.

Mai Chao

I call my elders over for an audience.

We interrogate,

find out if this White demon is

serious with my daughter.

I want to see his face closer,

make sure he can take care and provide for her.

The sky has no clouds today.

That is a good sign.

Mai Lia is crying because she is scared,

fearful not knowing what is going to happen

to our oldest daughter.

I never dreamed of sending my daughter away with a

White man.

I cannot shake the mere idea off my mind

like pepper burning

at the back of my throat.

After two hours of intense deliberating,

we decide

Josh is serious about his

marriage proposal,

make him promise

no harm ever come to our daughter,

then shake his hand

to welcome him to the family.

Josh is to present $5,000 in cash as

a promise and dowry to us.

The money is not for us to keep.

We use it to prepare for their wedding.

Later that night,

Mai Lia and I cry

when our children are in bed.

Our daughter is going to be an American,

a White woman.

I cannot help but mourn the loss of

my beloved Hmong daughter.

There is nothing we can do

but let her go.

Most importantly,

everyone is well and alive.

We reluctantly open our

jars of fireflies,

letting one at a time fly away,

into a strange world,

unaccustomed to us,

as we try desperately to hold on to what we can.

I am a man deeply rooted in tradition.

My job is to make sure traditions

get passed down

to the next generation.

I want to believe

my culture will live on forever.

Life in the villages seems long ago.

I remember my heart light as a feather,

real happiness,

filling me up,

and my troubles seem less painful.

I miss the old ways

when life was

easier

to understand.

Pa Ying: Mother.

Children want to make

their parents

proud,

not disappoint them if they can help it.

I want to pursue my dreams and

one day help them.

Life here is different.

Let us find our own voices in America.

Experience is the best teacher.

Give us the gift of choice,

the freedom to choose,

the opportunity to grow.

What if it is my fate?

Two people coming together,

united in love.

I fall in love with Josh's sweet personality,

gentle smile,

kind heart,

thoughtfulness like no other.

His laughter

chasing gloomy clouds away,

no strings attached.

I feel a happy ache

thumping in my chest,

thinking of him.

Little by little,

the fears and hurtful words harvested inside

disappear,

fog burning in sunshine.

I prepare for something superior,

bigger,

a future,

dreams becoming reality.

I am not just a mere girl to him.

He loves me just the way I am.

I do not have to pretend,

ask for permission,

manipulate love.

His affection is free and unconditional

like roots that grow

longer with passing time,

unlike the forced love that mother and father

created many moons ago.

Love with a price tag

comes and goes.

Being content is a state of mind;

everyone deserves to be happy, valued,

bring each other up,

no one falls down.

Instead,

their mean words of wisdom cut me down

each time I climb this mountain of life,

devastating,

destructive.

I can never reach the top.

I think about all the possible ways to

make this situation work for my family.

Every time

my thoughts drift back to Josh.

Am I too selfish to think of my hopes and dreams?

Should I give up and follow the path

my parents want me to travel?

My pillow is drenched in tears as

I lay in the dark,

deciding,

thinking,

what if...

I let my heart choose.

Night, day, year,

a sense of peace washes over my body,

no regret.

Josh,

the man I imagine spending my life with,

basking in love into old age.

Each time I reason with my parents,

they kick me with odious words and refuse to listen.

Their way or no way.

In the end,

I have to choose.

Through all the tangled messes and

damaging words,

I remember Mom and Dad's sacrifice,

all the hardship and pain

they endured to bring us to America.

One of the hardest choices I have to make is

to follow my heart because

I know it is the right thing to do.

They need to let me go,

honor my freewill,

let me live my life.

It seems like the old folks are

interested in the past,

fearful to acknowledge the future.

The uncivil lectures,

impolite advice,

and words of wisdom

from disgruntled people

speak reflections of their own unhappy lives.

Love is a force of nature that

cannot be demanded

like the stars, moon, or wind

to come and go.

Three years of fighting,

at times hiding,

they reluctantly cut me loose.

At a high price,

I am a stranger within my own home.

They see me as a loss to them,

to our family,

to the community.

Like being banished,

no blessing,

only ferocious words

sending a child into

the world of adulthood.

My mind is strong,

but I fall apart like a turbulent sea with

an approaching storm,

bringing raindrops to my eyes.

They are not good at forgetting,

forgiving,

or letting things go without a fight.

Hopefully,

some day they will understand my choices.

My life is ripped from all that I grew up with:

culture,

people,

family.

I cannot turn back

once I set it in motion.

The seasons of joy and sorrow intermingle until

our wedding day.

Summer, 2003:

My heart sings with mirth

the day both Mother and Father awkwardly

sit at the honor table.

Josh holding my hand tightly,

not leaving my sight.

For our first time,

both men and women sit at the same table and

share a meal of

celebration and love.

Uneasy and uncomfortable,

we are taking a baby step toward change,

rewriting our own lives and expectations

in a new land.

Men always eat first;

that is how it has been done,

a tradition.

At snail pace,

we are transforming our culture,

for all to live respectfully and equally.

Growing up,

I often imagine my mother

sitting at the honor table on my wedding day.

Today,

both Hmong and American people

commemorate and acknowledge

one another as family.

Like the Vietnam War,

an event that changed the way

the Hmong people live

forever.

Our wedding

joins both cultures,

a fusion of two

merging into one.

Love is beyond skin color,

a language that

all hearts recognize and know.

Love unites people.

My emotions feel like puffs of clouds that

dance lazily

on a clear blue sky.

All the heaviness of loss and guilt are lifted away.

Kashia,

you are a child

born of love.

One of my fireflies becoming a reality,

illuminating this world with beauty.

Now go and gather your own fireflies.

Kashia: Son.

National History Day Presentation, 2014:

The judges will be in the auditorium

in five minutes.

I am used to being watched by people when

playing basketball;

these judges do not make me nervous.

I can handle them,

I tell myself.

I practice my presentation a hundred times

in front of Mom and Dad.

Mrs. Vogler and Mrs. Sullivan

see me in action.

They love it!

Think.

Concentrate.

Why am I so nervous?

My project is meaningful and worthwhile.

I gained a new appreciation

for my culture

and heard the tragic stories of

Grandma and Grandpa.

What they tell me comes from their memories,

through word of mouth.

I am a new generation

who will continue

the art of storytelling.

Maybe in a new form,

like in visual arts, books, and videos.

The Internet

is changing

the way information is shared;

I have to speak the truth

to respect the living and

honor those who lost their lives.

I am grateful that

Grandma and Grandpa

opened their hearts to me.

My time is short.

I will act and perform

the Hmong experience

for my audience.

Our oral tradition lives on

through my new blood.

Someday,

we will tell our stories

to our children

about America.

Ten minutes is all I have

to share my understanding and

interpretation of the Hmong conflict.

When I am through,

the audience will have a good idea of

my research project.

Shhha...shhha...shhha...

I wear full traditional Hmong clothes.

My head is too large

because I inherited

my dad's genes,

so Grandma made a special hat

for my big brain.

I am wearing

Grandpa's vest and black velvet trousers too.

His vest has

French silver coins

stitched on it.

Any little movement makes the coins

sing gently,

which has been getting people's attention.

As I stand before the judges,

proudly dressed in

my traditional clothes,

I think about my mom.

No matter where I go or

what I do in life,

I have Hmong and American blood.

The cycle of life

continues through the knowledge and wisdom

the people I love

have given to me.

Shhha...shhha...shhha...

I am here today because of

Mom and Dad.

I think of her words:

"Kashia,

you are a child

born of love.

One of my fireflies becoming a reality,

illuminating this world with beauty.

Now go and gather your own fireflies."

I open my mouth to tell my family's story,

the journey of the Hmong people.

The fear in my heart melts like ice.

My voice strengthens

as words spill out

with pride and love for my cultures.

I am a new generation of Hmong,

a hybrid of Hmong and American,

and this is our story.

Mai Chao

Further Reading

Chan, S. (1994). *Hmong means free: Life in Laos and America.* Philadelphia: Temple University Press.

Goldfarb, M. (1982). *Fighters, refugees, and immigrants: A story of the Hmong.* Minneapolis: Carolrhoda Books.

Hamilton-Merritt, J. (1993). *Tragic mountains: The Hmong, the Americans, and the secret wars for Laos, 1942-1992.* Indiana: Indiana University Press.

Livo, N., & Cha, D. (1991). *Folk stories of the Hmong: Peoples of Laos, Thailand, and Vietnam.* Englewood, CO: Libraries Unlimited, Inc.

Long, L. (1992). *Ban Vinai: The refugee camp.* New York: Columbia University Press.

Millett, S. (2002). *The Hmong of Southeast Asia.* Minneapolis: Lerner Publications.

Moua, M. (2002). *Bamboo among the oaks: Contemporary writing by Hmong Americans.* Minneapolis: Minnesota Historical Society Press.

Murphy, N. (1997). *A Hmong family.* Minneapolis: Lerner Publications.

Quincy, K. (1988). *Hmong: History of a people.* Washington: Eastern Washington University Press.

Yang, D. (1993). *Hmong at the turning point* (1st ed.). Minneapolis: Worldbridge Associates Ltd.

ABOUT THE AUTHOR

Mai Chao is a Hmong-American artist, writer, and teacher. Her family came to the United States from a refugee camp when she was ten years old. She wrote this book in hopes of inspiring people to remember the past while honoring those who have paved the way for future generations. The time has come for Hmoob people to write their own histories and tell their own stories so they will be recorded authentically.

Mai Chao has lived happily in Wisconsin since her parents brought the family to America in 1992. She has two beautiful sons and a wonderful husband. Please feel free to email her at magentaspirit@gmail.com.